"I Think You've Accidentally Made an Enemy," Julie Said.

"But that's show biz. Come on. Don't worry about her. What's the point? Let's get changed."

Rena took a deep breath and walked a little faster. The air was so clean and fresh. The beautiful scenery helped to lift her spirits.

By the time the small dormitory came into view between the trees, she was feeling a lot better.

They went inside and walked quickly down the narrow corridor. "Julie, look. What's that?" Rena cried.

The door to their room was open. Two feet stuck out into the hallway—two sneakered feet.

Someone was lying facedown in the doorway.

Rena grabbed Julie's arm. On the carpet in front of the open door was a wide pool of dark red blood.

Books by R. L. Stine

Fear Street

THE NEW GIRL
THE SURPRISE PARTY
THE OVERNIGHT
MISSING
THE WRONG NUMBER
THE SLEEPWALKER
HAUNTED
HALLOWEEN PARTY
THE STEPSISTER
SKI WEEKEND
THE FIRE GAME
LIGHTS OUT
THE SECRET BEDROOM
THE KNIFE
PROM QUEEN
FIRST DATE
THE BEST FRIEND
THE CHEATER
SUNBURN
THE NEW BOY
THE DARE
BAD DREAMS
DOUBLE DATE
THE THRILL CLUB
ONE EVIL SUMMER
THE MIND READER

Fear Street Super Chiller

PARTY SUMMER
SILENT NIGHT
GOODNIGHT KISS
BROKEN HEARTS
SILENT NIGHT 2
THE DEAD LIFEGUARD

The Fear Street Saga

THE BETRAYAL
THE SECRET
THE BURNING

Fear Street Cheerleaders

THE FIRST EVIL
THE SECOND EVIL
THE THIRD EVIL

99 Fear Street: The House of Evil

THE FIRST HORROR
THE SECOND HORROR
THE THIRD HORROR

Other Novels

HOW I BROKE UP WITH ERNIE
PHONE CALLS
CURTAINS
BROKEN DATE

Available from ARCHWAY Paperbacks

CURTAINS

R. L. STINE

AN ARCHWAY PAPERBACK
Published by POCKET BOOKS

New York   London   Toronto   Sydney   Tokyo   Singapore

AN ARCHWAY PAPERBACK *Original*

An Archway Paperback published by
POCKET BOOKS, a division of Simon & Schuster Inc.
1230 Avenue of the Americas, New York, NY 10020

Copyright © 1990 by Bob Stine

ISBN: 0-671-69498-7

First Archway Paperback printing October 1990

15 14 13 12 11 10 9

AN ARCHWAY PAPERBACK and colophon are registered trademarks of Simon & Schuster Inc.

Cover illustration by Jeff Walker

Printed in the U.S.A.

IL 6+

Rena pulled out of his arms and jumped to her feet. "Don't touch me," she shouted, shivering with disgust.

Chip looked up at her from the worn green leather couch. For some reason he was smiling. It was a very inappropriate response.

Rena saw the smile. "How could you?" she asked in a low, trembling voice. She clenched her fists and stood poised over him, debating whether or not to hit him.

Finally she turned her back on him instead, her fists still clenched.

"What did I do?" he asked, his voice a nasal whine. He was trying to sound innocent, but the guilty smile had already given him away.

She didn't answer that. It wasn't worthy of a reply. Relaxing her fists, she ran both hands through her short sandy-blond hair. She didn't turn around.

"What did I *do?*" he repeated. The question

sounded even more insincere the second time around. He slapped the back of the couch with his big freckled fist.

She turned quickly and gazed down at him with more hatred than he had ever seen on her face before. "Andrea is my friend, my best friend," she said, forcing her voice to stay low and cool. "Did you really think you could come on to her without my knowing about it?"

His face filled with surprise. This look, too, wasn't terribly convincing. "She told you?"

"Yessss," Rena hissed. "She told me."

His face went blank. His green eyes narrowed. His freckled forehead wrinkled. He was thinking hard, thinking fast.

"So what?" he asked with an insolent shrug.

"So what? So *what?*" She felt herself go out of control. "How long have we been going together? How long?"

She glanced frantically around. What was she looking for?

"How can you say 'so what' to me after—after last week? The things we said—the things we *did* . . . So what? That's all that night was worth to you? So what?"

"Now, chill out, babes. Let's both just chill out." The desperation on her face told him he should be frightened.

He was right. He had gone too far this time.

She found what she was looking for. The knife was still on the sideboard, right where she had left it. She swept it into her hand, and with one quick motion— not enough time to think about it—she plunged the blade deep into his chest.

2

He didn't even scream.

His eyes rolled up in his head. He started to clutch his chest, but his arms fell to his sides, and he pitched forward, landing facedown on the floor with a loud thud.

She stared down at him for a few seconds and then raised her eyes to the ceiling. "Oh, Lord," she cried. "What have I done? What have I done?"

"Save that! Save that feeling!"

Rena heard Meritt Baxter shouting from the back of the small theater. "Save that feeling! That was very good."

Bax, as everyone called him, came bouncing up to the stage, clipboard in hand. "Very good. Very good, Rena. I'm impressed."

Rena's heart pounded. She realized she was grinning from ear to ear. She probably looked like a fool, but she didn't care.

Bax was impressed. This was quite a compliment coming from a real Broadway director. And it was the first compliment he had given her since camp had begun.

A few of the kids sprawled around the theater were applauding. Rena looked down at the seats, searching for Julie. When she spotted her in the third row, Julie raised her hand in an A-OK sign.

"I'm impressed," Bax repeated, pulling at his bushy white beard. His impressive deep voice boomed off the concrete walls. "It's a real start. With a lot of hard work, you could be extremely adequate."

Now Rena felt like a fool for grinning. She could feel her cheeks growing hot.

The compliment wasn't a compliment at all. That

was so like Bax, Rena thought. In the week since camp had started, he was always saying something that made one of them feel good, then quickly taking it away.

It was a game the camp director played with them, Rena realized, a cruel game. Bax might look like a jolly Santa Claus with his big belly, his pink cheeks, his baby-blue eyes that always seemed to be laughing, and his wild, unbrushed white hair and beard, but he was a complicated person. He had a mean streak. At least his sense of humor was mean. And his jokes always seemed to be aimed at kids onstage, when they were the most vulnerable.

"Hey, help me up!" Rena turned around at the sound of the voice. Chip was still lying on the floor, the collapsible knife in his hand. "The least you can do after killing me is help me up."

Rena laughed. Chip was such a clown. She took his big hand and pulled. He climbed to his feet and brushed the dust from his jeans. "Thanks. Wow! Your hands are ice-cold."

"I get so nervous," Rena confided. "I've never been on a stage before in my life, unless you count third grade. And I certainly never thought I'd be acting in front of a famous Broadway director."

"You did great," Chip said.

Rena smoothed her hair with both hands. It was a nervous habit—one she couldn't break. She seldom realized she was doing it. "You were good too," she said. "I loved your fall. You looked like you were really dead."

"Aw, shucks," Chip said with exaggerated modesty. "Actually, I learned how to play dead by watching my dog." He barked a few times, twisting up his face so that he really looked like a dog.

He's a natural actor, Rena thought. It's all so easy for him. And it's all such hard work for me. What am I doing up here?

Rena turned back to the front of the stage. The kids in the audience were laughing and talking, mostly about the performance she and Chip had just given.

"People! People, if I can have your attention," Bax called loudly. "You can make your plans later for sneaking out after lights-out. I hope I assume correctly that the reason you have chosen to spend your summer at the Meritt Baxter Summer Theater Camp is that you are slightly more interested in learning about theater than in learning about the opposite sex."

This got a pretty good laugh. Then everyone quickly became quiet. No one wanted Bax to lose his temper, the way he had on the first day of camp.

Rena and Chip walked to the apron of the stage and sat down, letting their legs dangle over the side. Bax was pacing back and forth in front of them, observing the kids in the audience.

"Let's talk a little bit about what we've just seen up there," Bax said, tapping the clipboard against his right leg. "Rena, you did some marvelous things with your hands," he said, narrowing his blue eyes as he stared up into hers. "I loved the thing you did, sweeping your hands through your hair. I could feel the tension."

"Thank you, sir," Rena said, a little embarrassed to be complimented for something she did all the time.

"Bax. Call me Bax," he said, still staring at her without blinking. "The hands were good, Rena. But

5

you have to be careful not to go over the top when you want to increase the intensity."

"Over the top? What do you mean?"

"Well, you rolled your eyes to the ceiling after you stabbed Chuck."

"Chip. It's Chip," Chip corrected.

Bax looked down at his clipboard. "Sorry, my friend. Perhaps we shall change your name to Chuck, since I keep calling you that."

He turned back to Rena. "Lose the eye rolling," he told her. "And you overdid the clenched fists too. If you turn your back to the audience, I want to see the tension in your back, I want to feel it in your back, not in your fists. Do you think you can do that?"

"I'll try," Rena said uncertainly. She glanced at Julie in the third row, who made a face at her.

"What is your story, Rena?" Bax asked, suddenly hopping up onto the stage. It was a startling move for someone so fat. "Did you want to be an actress all your life? Is that why you've come to my theater camp?"

"No," Rena answered quickly, surprised by the personal question. It was the first personal question he had asked anyone all week. "My friend Julie talked me into coming."

Rena could hear Julie groaning three rows away.

Bax shook his head and pulled on his beard. "Well, maybe we can turn you into an actress anyway," he said. "You just might surprise yourself, Rena. You just might have some talent."

"Thank you," Rena said, embarrassed by all the attention.

"That's why I've decided to give you the lead in our play," Bax added casually.

The lead?

Did she hear right? Did he just say she had won the lead?

Was it another one of his jokes?

No. The serious look on his face indicated that he meant it.

"Oh, thank you!" Rena cried. She didn't know what else to say. For a second she had the urge to jump up and hug him. But she wasn't the type of person to get carried away like that. Even when she was this happy.

At last, she told herself, something good has happened in my life. Finally—after the past three horrible years—something I can be proud of.

"And, Chuck, you will play the role of Andrew," Bax announced.

Before Chip could remind Bax that his name wasn't Chuck, they were interrupted by an angry cry from the back of the theater. "Now, wait a minute, Bax!"

Hedy came storming up to the stage, her long auburn hair flowing behind her in rippled torrents like a waterfall, her dark lipsticked mouth turned down in anger. In the week since camp had begun, Hedy had proved to be not only the most dramatic-looking person in camp but also the most dramatic in temperament.

She pulled Bax to the side of the stage, her green eyes flashing angrily. "I'm supposed to be the lead, Bax. That role was promised to me!" Hedy exclaimed in a low voice, just loud enough so Rena could hear every word.

"I made no such promise," Rena heard Bax say, his face expressionless.

"My mother didn't pay all this money for me to spend the summer painting scenery while this—this

7

amateur plays the lead!" Hedy shouted, too angry and out of control now to care if everyone heard her.

Rena couldn't hear Bax's quiet reply. But whatever he said made Hedy even angrier.

Since the moment camp had begun and they had all been ushered into the small theater and told about the production of Bax's play *Curtains*, the play they would be working on all summer, Hedy had made it clear to everyone that her mother expected her to be the star, expected her eventually to be taken to Broadway as Bax's discovery.

A lot of the kids, Rena had learned, had fantasies about being discovered by Bax. They came to his camp with glorious dreams of how they would overwhelm the veteran director with their talent, and how the camp would be the starting place of a long career as stars in the theater.

Rena, of course, had no such fantasies. She had no burning desire to be an actress. She had never even thought about it. Rena just came to the camp because Julie had convinced her it would be fun.

Sometimes during the week of tryouts and getting acquainted, Rena had actually felt sorry for Hedy. The fantasy of being a Broadway star didn't seem to be Hedy's. It seemed to be her mother's.

But now, with Hedy ranting and raving, swinging her long red hair back and forth as she paced, it was hard to feel sorry for her.

"I know why you gave her the part!" Hedy was shrieking, pointing contemptuously at Rena. "You gave her the part because she looks like Michelle Pfeiffer! That's what everyone has been saying all week. Doesn't she look like Michelle Pfeiffer! Michelle Pfeiffer! So what, Bax? So what? She can't act, and you know it! I can! You've seen me act. You can't give the part to her. You can't!"

"Okay, okay," Bax said, raising his hands as if surrendering. "You win, Hedy. You get the part." He turned apologetically to Rena. "Sorry, Rena."

Rena stared back at him in disbelief. "But you can't—" She couldn't finish her sentence. Was he really cruel enough to do that to her?

Bax returned her stare, an odd little smile spreading across his face. He must have seen the hurt and humiliation on her face. Why was he smiling?

"Just kidding," he told her. He turned back to Hedy. "Did you really think you could make me change my mind by throwing a tantrum in front of everyone?"

Hedy was too furious to reply.

"Your sense of drama is good, but your sense of timing is abysmal," Bax told Hedy. "Now, go back to your seat. I've given you the best character part. The mother. I know you can do wonderful things with it."

"I'm not playing the mother!" Hedy said through clenched teeth. "I'm playing the lead!"

"My dear Miss Franklyn," Bax said, raising himself up to his full height, his voice booming once again, "there may be a place for such callow histrionics in show business, but there is no place for them in the theater!"

That declaration was meant to end the discussion. But Hedy was not finished. She turned away from Bax and walked over to Rena. She leaned down, putting her mouth right up to Rena's ear, and whispered, "You'll never play that part. Never. I'll make you sorry you ever stepped on a stage. And that's a promise!"

Rena gasped out loud without realizing it. Hedy really seemed to mean what she said. Rena could feel Hedy's hot breath against her ear, could hear the whispered threat again and again even after Hedy jumped off the stage.

Hedy hurried up the aisle toward the exit. Bax hopped down from the stage and bounced after her. "Hedy, stop right there! Stop!"

She disappeared out the door. He followed her, calling after her the whole way.

The kids in the audience, who had sat through Hedy's tantrum in shocked and embarrassed silence, burst into nervous laughter and chatter. Rena and Chip jumped down from the stage. Rena felt strange. Her head was spinning. Hedy's angry words would not go away. "You'll never play that part. Never!"

"Don't pay any attention to her," Chip said, putting a hand on her shoulder. It felt hot and wet against her T-shirt. "She was being overdramatic."

"I think she meant what she said," Rena told him.

"No. You're just not used to theater people," he insisted. "They carry on like hurricanes. But it's only wind." He puffed up his freckled cheeks and blew.

Julie came rushing up to Rena and gave her a quick hug. "You were great up there!" she cried. "Don't sweat Hedy. She'll get over it. You know, I'm jealous. If I'd known you were this good, I wouldn't have convinced you to come!"

Rena forced a laugh. It was sweet of Julie to try to cheer her up.

"You were good too," Julie told Chip. She lowered

her head and gazed up at him with dark, soulful eyes. When she did that, she looked just like Cher. So she did it a lot. "I have to tell you that I really get turned on by guys with red hair and freckles. Does that make you uncomfortable?"

"No. Of course not," Chip said uncomfortably. He took a step back. She was practically standing on his sneakers.

"If you need someone to rehearse with—you know, at nights—I'm available," Julie said with a meaningful smile.

She never quits, Rena thought, admiring Julie's boldness.

"Thanks," Chip said. He quickly turned back to Rena.

"Actually, I thought you and I could go for a swim later. Maybe talk about the roles and—"

Before Rena could reply, Bax burst back into the theater—without Hedy. "People! People!" he called. He didn't look angry, but his face was still bright red. "Seats, everyone! Could we have quiet, please. We still have a lot of work to do today."

Kids scrambled back to their seats. The theater quickly became quiet.

"Let's rehearse the scene where George catches you with Chuck—er, Chip," Bax told Rena.

Chip and Rena climbed back onto the stage.

"George? Where's George?" Bax called, sounding very annoyed. "Is *everyone* walking out today? George, are you here?"

Silence. George was not in the theater.

"Okay, that's it," Bax said. He threw both hands high above his head and tossed the clipboard to the floor. It clattered noisily on the concrete. "Why don't you all go for a swim?" he said, exasperated. "We're not going to get any work done today."

Someone in the back of the theater cheered and got an extremely annoyed look from Bax.

"Go ahead. Go," he insisted. "Have a swim. This is a camp, after all. We do have that lovely beach all to ourselves on the sound. Oh, one last thing, campers—"

Rena had to chuckle. The way he said the word *campers* made them sound like some sort of lower life form.

"Let me warn you again. Please, please stay away from the old boathouse on the dock. I heard that some of you were in there the other day. It's really quite dangerous. It's falling apart. The whole dock may be collapsing, as far as I know. And when the tide comes in, the boathouse gets almost entirely submerged. So please—please—I know it's an inviting setting for amorous encounters. But please confine those to the bushes and stay away from the rotting old boathouse. End of warning."

He picked up the clipboard, slapped it loudly against his leg as a signal of dismissal, turned, and headed toward the exit.

"Hey, how about that swim?" Chip asked Rena.

"A swim is a great idea," Julie said, stepping between them. "I'm sweating like a pig. I didn't think New Hampshire got this hot in July. We should be doing *Cat on a Hot Tin Roof* or some sultry Tennessee Williams play where everyone walks around in T-shirts and sweats out their emotional hang-ups." She put a hand on Chip's big shoulder. "I'm feeling kinda sultry today. How about you, Chip?"

"No. Just hot," Chip said, looking more uncomfortable. "You're really into theater, aren't you?"

"Yes." Julie looked flattered. "How could you tell?"

"The way you talk, I guess."

"All Julie ever talks about is theater," Rena said. (To herself she added, "Theater and boys.") "She's a really good actress."

"That's why I'm playing the maid, and you've got the lead role," Julie said, trying to keep it light, but a little bitterness slipped into her voice. "You'll probably wow everyone when we perform it the last week of camp, and Bax will beg you to open on Broadway as his own personal discovery."

"For sure, Julie. Then I'll run for president and fly to Mars!"

"Don't laugh, Rena. Bax is still an important theater person," Julie said seriously, eyeing Chip as she talked to Rena. "Sure, he hasn't had a hit for ten years, but people remember him, people still respect his opinion. You wouldn't be the first talented young actress to be discovered in this camp."

"For sure," Rena repeated, rolling her eyes. Then she remembered Bax telling her to lose the eye rolling.

"Why'd you come to this camp?" Julie asked Chip.

"To meet girls," he said, grinning. His cheeks turned bright pink. "Come on, how about that swim?"

"We'll meet you down at the sound in five minutes," Julie said, blowing a wisp of dark hair off her face.

"Okay, I guess . . ." Rena said, even though she didn't really feel like it.

Chip hurried off toward the boys' dorm up the hill from the theater. Julie pulled Rena toward their dorm, which was tucked among a clump of thick pine trees on the far side of the hill. It was a low, flat-roofed, gray-shingled building that resembled a motel more than a dormitory.

"I just can't stop thinking about Hedy," Rena told her friend. "Did you see the way she looked at me? Such hatred? I didn't do anything to her. I don't even know her!"

"Yeah. I think you've made an enemy," Julie said rather matter-of-factly. "But that's show biz. Come on. Don't worry about her. What's the point? Let's get changed."

They walked up the dirt path and turned toward the dorm. A soft breeze carried the fresh fragrance of pine. Tiny black-and-white chickadees darted from tree to tree, chattering noisily. Beyond the trees stretched the low green mountains New Hampshire was famous for.

Rena took a deep breath and walked a little faster. The air was so clean and fresh. The beautiful scenery helped to lift her spirits.

By the time the small dormitory came into view among the trees, she was feeling a lot better.

They went inside and walked quickly down the narrow corridor. "Julie, look. What's that?" Rena cried.

The door to their room was open. Two feet stuck out into the hallway, two sneakered feet.

Someone was lying face down in the doorway.

Rena grabbed Julie's arm. On the carpet in front of the open door was a wide pool of dark red blood.

2

The girls crept close enough to see that the shoes protruding from the doorway were yellow Keds. One of them was untied, the laces trailing into the pool of blood, which had spread over the carpet in a perfect oval shape.

"Don't touch anything," Rena warned, still holding on to Julie's arm.

"Don't worry," Julie said, feeling as if she might be sick at any moment. "We'd better get help."

Rena peered bravely into the doorway. "Oh, no," she said, the words coming out in a whisper. "It's— George."

"Is he—dead?" Julie asked, her voice tiny, almost a squeak. She couldn't take her eyes off the dark pool of blood.

Dead.

Dead.

The word carried Rena back.

Suddenly she was no longer standing in a shadowy dormitory hallway, staring at the body of a boy she had met only a few days before.

Suddenly she was back three years in time, staring at the body of—staring at the boy she knew—staring at the boy who—staring at the boy she thought she—

"Rena, are you okay? Rena!"

Julie's frightened cries brought Rena back.

This can't be happening, she thought. I can't let this happen.

"NO! NO! NO!" The screams burst out of her as if she had no control over them, as if they were coming from somewhere else, some place long buried within her. "NO! NO! THIS CAN'T BE HAPPENING!"

The yellow Keds moved.

George rolled over and sat up. "Okay. If you insist," he said, grinning. "You don't have to shout."

Both girls jumped back. Rena's mouth formed a wide *O* of surprise, but no sound came out.

Still grinning, enjoying their reaction immensely, George climbed to his feet.

"Gotcha!" he said. He began to laugh, a wide, toothy laugh, his narrow shoulders shaking, his large black eyes dancing in merriment.

Rena and Julie stared at him without moving.

"You're not dead!" Julie said, almost accusingly.

"No. I'm not even sick!" he exclaimed, and began laughing all over again.

"The blood isn't real either," Rena told Julie. She scraped her finger through it. Stage blood.

They waited for him to stop laughing.

"Why'd you do it?" Julie asked.

He shrugged. Then he bent down to tie his sneaker.

He was wearing faded jean cutoffs and a sleeveless gray T-shirt. The T-shirt was also stained with dark red stage blood.

The old memories, the old horrors, weaved in and out of Rena's mind. She struggled to push them away, struggled to stay in the present.

George took his time tying his sneaker. He tried to wipe the red blood off the laces, but it wouldn't budge.

Rena stared down at him, concentrating, willing the old memories away. He's kind of cute, she thought. With his dark eyes and even darker, short spiky hair, he looked a lot like a movie star Rena liked—Matt Dillon. He even smiles like Matt Dillon, Rena thought.

"George, that was a real Mickey Mouse stunt you pulled," Julie said angrily.

"Yeah. Why'd you do it, George?" Rena asked. Her heartbeat was finally returning to its normal rhythm.

He gave Rena his slowest and best Matt Dillon smile. "I was just trying to make an impression," he said.

"You made an impression," Julie said sarcastically. "A bad one." She blew a wisp of black curly hair from over her eye.

He ignored Julie. He kept his smile on Rena. "I've been trying to get your attention all week, but you've been ignoring me."

"I didn't know—" Rena started.

"You'll have to admit it got your attention. I'm the prop master, so I can get fake blood and all kinds of great stuff," he said with some pride. His dark eyes burned into Rena's.

He's so intense, she thought. He's like an excited little boy. He seems so—so—needy.

"I can get scars, bullet wounds—anything! It's terrific!"

"Yeah. Terrific," Julie said scathingly. "So you get off on scaring people, huh?"

"I don't think that performing should be confined to the stage," George said, still staring at Rena. "Have you read much about performance art?"

"You think lying in a pool of stage blood in our doorway trying to scare us to death is art?" Julie asked angrily, her hands on her hips.

"Yes. I try to create an artistic situation, with myself as the subject," George said. "I think I can evoke the same feelings a painter might, or a sculptor, or even a playwright, by using myself to create a fictitious scene in the middle of a real-life situation."

"Come off it," Julie said. "You just wanted us to lose our lunch when we saw you."

"That would have been a legitimate response," George said in all seriousness. He smiled at Rena.

"It's a good thing you're such a fox," Julie said, her anger fading quickly. "If you weren't so cute, you couldn't get away with garbage like that."

He seemed to be really offended. "Art isn't cute," he said flatly.

Julie reached out and brushed some dirt off George's shirt.

"Are you going to be an actor?" Rena asked.

The question seemed to surprise him. "Bax thinks I show promise," he replied.

He made Rena feel really strange. Most boys Rena knew didn't stare into her eyes like that. It was almost as if he was challenging her to stare back, to meet his intensity.

She glanced down at the carpet.

"Rena and I are going for a swim," Julie said. "Want to meet us down there?"

"Yes. That would be great," he said.

"No. I—uh—I've changed my mind," Rena said to Julie. "I think I'm going to lie down for a while."

Julie looked annoyed for a second; then she brightened. "Okay. Then I'll meet you down at the water," she told George.

"No. Some other time," George said.

Julie tried to hide it, but she looked hurt.

George stepped past them and began ambling down the hallway.

"See you around," Julie called after him.

He stopped and turned around. "If there's anything I can do for you, let me know," he said, looking only at Rena. He seemed to put extra meaning in the words. They were an unmistakable invitation.

"What about the blood?" Rena called. The pool of blood was troubling her even though she knew it was fake.

George shrugged. "It'll wash right out. It's water-soluble," he said. He gave her a short wave. "Art and illusion," he added mysteriously. "That's what we're all here for, right? Art and illusion . . ."

They watched him lope away until he disappeared around the corner. Then they stepped over the pool of red and went into their room.

It was small, and the painted plasterboard walls were thin. They could hear girls talking and moving around in the rooms on both sides of theirs. It's sort of like living inside an egg carton, Rena had thought when she first moved in.

There was only room enough for a bunk bed, a wooden folding chair, and a single dresser with a small rectangular mirror above it. The dresser was knotty pine, and it took a magician or a muscleman to open the drawers, which were warped and smelled of mildew. There was a closet the size of a phone booth. The single window faced down the hill toward the sound. The bathroom was at the end of the hall.

"He's a real babe," Julie said, plopping down onto the chair.

Rena made a face.

Julie looked surprised. "He sure seemed interested in you."

"I don't care," Rena said wearily, lying down on the bottom bunk, Julie's bed. "He's not my type."

"Not your type?"

"He's too intense. Too—crazy. Lying on the floor, pretending to be dead. That's sick."

"It was just a joke," Julie said, surprised at Rena's vehement reaction.

"And I didn't like the way he stared into my eyes like some sort of mad hypnotist," Rena said.

"You're just not used to theater people. He was only being dramatic. Hey, you really don't look well. You got so pale."

"Oh, I'll be all right. It's just that he—well, he brought back some memories."

"Memories? Something you've been keeping from me? Come on, Rena, spill!"

Rena didn't smile. Julie realized she had made a mistake by making a joke. She picked up a hairbrush and began pulling it quickly through her tangles of black hair. The more she brushed, the more unruly and wild her hair became.

Rena stared up at the top bunk. She was angry at herself for revealing why she was upset. She didn't want to discuss it with Julie. She *couldn't* discuss it with Julie. So what had made her mention it?

"Before I moved to Cambridge," she started, speaking slowly, carefully, her voice no more than a whisper, "before I met you—something terrible happened. I've never wanted to tell you about it." She was silent for a moment, then added, "I still don't."

Julie didn't reply. She kept brushing her hair, staring at the floor. Two girls in the room on the other side of the dresser were laughing loudly.

After a while Julie said, "Maybe that's why you've been so good in the play. Maybe you've been using your memories, drawing on them to help you perform."

"I don't know," Rena said, still staring up at the mattress over her head. She was relieved that Julie wasn't going to force her to say more. She would much rather talk about the play than about—the memories.

"You were so good at rehearsal today, so angry, I really believed it when you stabbed Chip. Did you hear me shriek?"

Rena smiled. "I guess I got a little carried away."

"It was great. You'd better get carried away every day," Julie told her. "Bax really seemed impressed."

"Bax seems to like stabbing," Rena said. "I get the feeling that beneath his jolly Santa Claus exterior there's an ax murderer waiting to get out."

Julie dropped her hairbrush. "Come off it, Rena. What are you saying?"

"I'm saying that I think Bax is a cruel person."

"Well, I don't think Bax is cruel. *Curtains* is a cruel play. I just think he wants to get all of the emotion out of us that he can."

"Get real, Julie. What about on the first day of

camp? How he made us all get into our bathing suits and walk around on the stage in them and stare at each other, looking each other up and down? And we didn't even know each other."

"He was trying to open us up, Rena. It was a dramatic way to get us over our shyness."

"It was cruel. And what about two days ago when he made us team up and then make cracks about each other's appearance? That was horrible."

"That's a valid theatrical technique, Rena. Bax wasn't just doing it for kicks."

"Oh, no? Well, did you check out his face? Did you see how much he was enjoying watching us tear each other to pieces? Poor Marcie—that really short girl with the bad skin—she was in tears. And Bax just laughed. He wouldn't stop it. He *wanted* her to cry."

"Maybe he did. But not out of cruelty. Being able to cry onstage is a very valuable technique to learn, Rena." Julie bent down to pick up her hairbrush and tossed it onto the dresser. "Oh, why do I have to defend Bax anyway?" she asked, exasperated. "He's a famous director. He knows what he's doing. You're just new to all this."

"Maybe," Rena said, sitting up suddenly. "But even a Martian could see that he really enjoys embarrassing us and making us feel uncomfortable."

"Well, you don't have to feel uncomfortable anymore. You got the lead role," Julie said with just a hint of bitterness. She quickly changed the subject. "How about changing your mind and coming for that swim? It would revive you. Really."

"Oh, I don't know. . . ." What Rena really wanted was to curl up in a ball and escape into a long, peaceful nap.

Julie walked over to the dresser, struggled with the top drawer, finally managed to pull it open a couple of inches, and took out a tiny blue-and-white bikini. "Well, if you make up your mind . . ." She tossed her clothes onto the floor of the tiny closet and put on the bathing suit.

"Very sexy bathing suit," Rena said, admiring Julie's boldness. Rena knew she'd never go out in public in a bathing suit that tiny.

"You think so?" Julie said, pleased by the compliment. "You think Chip will like it?"

"Chip? I *thought* I saw that look in your eye when you met him," Rena teased.

"Well, it's just that he looks so much like Danny," Julie said.

Danny.

Rena froze at the sound of his name.

How could Julie mention him so casually?

3

"Stop that, Rena," Julie said harshly, walking over to the window. "You don't have to get all crazy if I mention Danny."

"I didn't—" Rena started.

"I'm completely over Danny. And I'm completely over the fact that—" Julie hesitated.

"That I took Danny away from you? Is that what you started to say?"

Rena lay back on the lower bunk and stared at the wall. She didn't want this talk, didn't want to confront Julie on this subject. She wanted it buried, buried in the past—with the other memories.

Julie shook her hair out of her face. "You didn't take Danny from me," she said quietly.

Rena turned back to face her. She could see that Julie wasn't going to stop. Julie was determined to discuss Danny. Rena took a deep breath. I guess it had to happen sooner or later, she told herself.

"You didn't take Danny from me," Julie repeated, watching the tall pines through the window. "That's what I realized this spring. It was all Danny. Danny chose to drop me and go out with you. You didn't force him. You didn't even want to, at first. Right?"

"Well—yes," Rena said, embarrassed. Yes, it had happened. Yes, it had ruined their friendship. Yes, they hadn't spoken for months.

Yes, yes, yes.

Why did they have to talk about it all now?

"At first I thought I'd never forgive you," Julie said, still staring out the window. "I was so hurt. And so angry. But then I realized I was directing my anger at the wrong person. It was Danny I was angry at. It was Danny who had hurt me. It was Danny who had rejected me, who had made all the choices. Not you. I guess somehow it was easier to be angry at you, easier than confronting my real feelings."

"Well, he's dropped both of us now," Rena said bitterly, staring up at the mattress above her head.

Julie laughed. "I guess that's what made me feel close to you again."

"What? What did you say?"

"I said, I think that's what made me feel close to you again. When Danny broke up with you too, we had something in common. I wasn't angry anymore. I felt you and I could really be good friends again. Closer than before."

Rena laughed. Nervous laughter. The whole discussion was making her very uncomfortable. She didn't want to hear any explanations or confessions from Julie.

She knew that Julie had been furious with her when

she started going out with Danny. And, of course, she remembered how bitterly the friendship had ended because of it. Rena also remembered that a few months later—after Danny had broken up with her too—Julie had suddenly reappeared in her life and they had slowly begun to rebuild the close friendship they had had.

What more was there to discuss?

"That's when I got the idea of our going away to camp together," Julie was saying. "It seemed like a great way to really repair our friendship. Spending so much time together and letting it all hang out. You know, our true feelings."

"Right," Rena said blankly. She wasn't the kind of person who let her true feelings hang out. She was private. She liked to keep things to herself, work things out in her own mind.

I'm not like these kids who are into theater, Rena thought. They always have to be talking about their feelings, grabbing people, touching people, talking, talking, living their lives out in public. Julie and George and Hedy—they all seem so needy.

The sun went behind a cloud, and the room suddenly grew dark.

Rena waited for Julie to say more about Danny. But she didn't.

"I'd better get down to the water," Julie said, walking quickly to the closet, bending down, and searching the floor for a towel. "The weather changes so quickly here. I'll miss the sun. And I told Chip we'd be down—"

Now that she had said what she'd planned to, Julie wanted to change the subject. She never really wanted

26

to discuss Danny, Rena realized. It was like a little performance—a clear-the-air speech. She had probably rehearsed it for a long time.

"You've been a good friend," Rena said suddenly.

Julie turned around, surprised.

"No. I mean it," Rena said. "What you just said—about Danny. That was really nice of you. And you didn't even get angry or jealous when I got the lead in *Curtains* and you're playing the maid."

"Let's not get all sloppy sentimental about this," Julie said. She stared hard at Rena, as if trying to see into her brain. "I got plenty jealous," Julie said, swinging a pink towel over her shoulder. "Who do you think you are, anyway!"

Rena laughed. "I'm serious."

"Me too," Julie said.

"Oh." Rena grabbed her forehead.

Something had dripped on her. "Hey!" She felt another wet drip, this time on her arm.

It couldn't be rain, she realized. Whatever it was felt warm. Besides, it was bright sunshine outside once again.

Rena rolled out of the lower bunk to investigate.

"What's the matter?" Julie asked.

"Something's dripping from the top bunk," Rena told her.

The drips were dark red.

"What on earth—"

Rena stepped on the bottom bunk so that she could see up on her bed.

"Oh, good Lord!"

Something bulged under her blanket. The khaki blanket was drenched, now wine-colored with blood.

Dark red blood had soaked through the mattress and was now dripping through to the bunk below.

"Julie—" She fought off the wave of nausea that choked her throat. "Julie, there's blood. And—I think this time it's real."

4

What was under the blanket?

Rena's knees went weak. She felt dizzy. Gripping the frame of the top bunk tightly, she waited for her head to clear.

"What is it? What is it?" Julie was calling. She sounded so far away.

"What is it? Rena, what is it?" Julie could have been a million miles away, but she was standing right next to Rena. She had climbed up onto the bed too.

Rena stared at the dark, wet blood.

Was this another prank?

Something told her it wasn't.

There was only one way to find out.

She took a deep breath, held it. Grasping the bunk frame with her left hand, she reached out for the top of the blanket.

"No! Don't!" Julie cried.

Rena didn't seem to hear her.

With a quick, decisive tug, she pulled back the blanket.

Both girls gasped when they saw it.

It was a swan, probably one of the swans that had lived in the sound.

Its eyes were rolled back in its head. Its beak lay open. Its neck was bent at an odd angle. Its throat had been slit, a long, deep cut at least three inches long.

Blood lay in a pool around the slit in the neck, seeping into the matted white feathers of the dead creature's arched body, soaking into Rena's sheet and mattress, so red, so blood-red.

Julie jumped down first. "Rena, get down. Rena, can you hear me?"

The blood. All the blood. As Rena stared, she was no longer in the tiny dormitory room. She was back, back home, back with the blood of three years ago, Kenny's blood, so red, so blood-red.

She couldn't take her eyes off it.

It was everywhere.

It couldn't be his blood—could it?

All that blood. All that time ago. And here it was again. Here was the blood. Kenny's blood, following her, following her, following her, following her, following her, following her . . .

"RENA—GET DOWN!"

Julie pulled her away.

She fell back, back, but the blood stayed in front of her eyes.

She fell on top of Julie. Both girls sprawled on the floor.

"Rena, are you okay? Ow! Get off me!"

Julie's cries brought Rena back. She realized she had fallen on top of Julie. "Sorry. Really. I'm so sorry." She pulled herself to her feet, felt dizzy, sat back down on the floor.

They both sat there for a while, not looking at each other.

"Did I hurt you?" Rena asked finally.

"No. I'm okay," Julie said. "But I had to pull you down. You were hypnotized or something up there."

"I—uh—I don't know." Rena didn't know what to say. It was taking all her concentration to stay in the present. She didn't want to go back to the past.

But she didn't want to stay in the present either.

"That swan. It's—"

"I don't believe Hedy," Julie scowled. She shook her curly hair out of her eyes.

"Hedy?"

Rena was concentrating, concentrating.

It wasn't his blood. It isn't his blood. It's a swan. It's just a swan. It's today. It isn't then.

"That Hedy's real subtle, isn't she? How disgusting!"

Julie climbed to her feet and started pacing the small room nervously. "Hey, are you going to be all right?"

"Yeah. Sure. I guess," Rena said doubtfully. "Yeah. I feel better. It's just—"

"She must've sneaked in here after she stormed out of rehearsal," Julie said, biting her lower lip. "Can you believe it? Does she really think this is going to get her the lead role? Does she think you're going to go running home to your mommy or something just because she put a dead swan in your bed?"

"Maybe." Rena didn't know what to think. "Do you really think Hedy could kill a swan like that? Just slit its throat?"

"Don't you?" Julie demanded, pacing faster. "Of course she did. She probably didn't use a knife. She probably used her fingernail!"

"Julie, I—"

"How disgusting. How low can you get? Killing an innocent bird. And what silly, juvenile symbolism. It's—it's so—babyish!"

"She got her point across," Rena muttered. She looked down at her hand. It was smeared with dark blood. The blood was starting to cake.

"No, I didn't do it!" she started to scream. She tried to rub the blood off, but it wouldn't come.

"What?" Julie stopped pacing. "What did you say?"

"What?" Rena hadn't heard herself scream. "Nothing. I didn't say anything."

"Yes, you did. You said—" Julie stopped. She could see that Rena was very upset. She decided it wasn't a good time for any kind of argument or discussion.

"What are we going to do now?" Rena moaned.

"We're not going to let her get away with this, are we?" Julie studied Rena's pale white face. She was trying to determine just how troubled Rena was. But the face hid much more than it revealed.

"No," Rena replied, but without much conviction. "We can't. But what can we do?" It was more of a plea than a question.

"We'll kill something larger and put it in her bed!" Julie declared. "Did you ever see *The Godfather*? Maybe we'll get a horse!"

Still seated on the floor, Rena hugged her legs and buried her head in them.

"Just kidding," Julie said. "Just trying to keep it light."

"Light," Rena repeated weakly.

32

"Well, what should we do?" Julie asked herself. "I guess we should go and tell Bax."

"Oh, for sure," Rena said sarcastically. "That'll do a lot of good. You know what he'd say? 'Hold that feeling! Save that emotion!' You know what? Bax probably put the swan in my bed—to open up my feelings!"

Julie laughed. Then she realized that Rena wasn't kidding.

"Get real. Bax owns this camp, remember. He's not going to run around killing swans and stuffing them into kids' beds in his own camp. I know you think he's cruel, Rena. But he isn't *that* cruel! And he isn't crazy."

"You're sure about that?" Rena asked, but she realized she was just stalling. She didn't want to get up and clean up the mess. And mainly, she didn't want to face the fact that another girl—a girl she had just met a few days earlier—hated her enough to do this cruel thing, hated her enough to kill another living creature.

She climbed slowly to her feet. There was a knock on the door. Both girls shrieked. Julie, in her tiny bathing suit, was covered with goose bumps.

"Who is it?" Rena called.

"Marcie. I heard screaming in there. Is everything okay?"

Julie pulled open the door. "Hi, Marcie. Come in. Everything isn't exactly okay, would you say, Rena?"

"Not exactly," Rena said.

Marcie came in, acting bewildered. She was very short, five feet tall at the most, and she had short brown hair on a tiny round head. She reminded Rena of a cartoon mouse. She even spoke in a squeaky, high-pitched voice.

"What's wrong?" Marcie asked, not venturing far into the room.

"There was an accident," Julie told her, pointing to the top bunk. "Would you believe that a swan flew in the window and committed suicide in Rena's bunk?"

"No. I don't think so," Marcie said uncertainly.

"Well, go take a look," Julie said, unable to suppress a devilish grin.

Marcie took a few steps toward the bunk.

"NO!" Rena cried, and held her back. "Julie, it isn't funny. Why should she be upset too?"

Julie shrugged.

"There really is a dead swan in there," Rena told Marcie. "Its throat was slashed. Someone put it in there to—to scare me, I guess."

"How awful," Marcie said, staring up at the bunk. "Who could have done it?"

"We think it was you," Julie joked.

Marcie just stared at her. Then she forced a laugh, a high-pitched giggle, when she realized Julie was joking.

"My sense of humor always comes out at the worst times," Julie admitted.

"You look just like Cher," Marcie said suddenly. "Did anyone ever tell you that? She has a funny sense of humor too."

"Thanks. I guess," Julie said. You look just like Minnie Mouse, she thought. She scolded herself for being so mean-natured.

"We've got to get the blood out of here," Rena interrupted. "So much blood today. Real blood. Fake blood." She felt herself slipping back again.

"I'll help," Marcie volunteered. "Are you okay, Rena? Rena?"

It took a while for Rena to realize that Marcie was talking to her. "Yeah. Fine. Thanks, Marcie."

The girls wrapped the swan up in the bloody sheets. All three of them carried it to a trashcan behind the dorm and stuffed it in.

It took a lot of cleaning and scrubbing and mopping to get the blood up. After nearly an hour, all but a few of the stains had been removed.

Rena carefully made up the new mattress with clean sheets. "Good as new. Almost," she said, forcing a smile.

"Are you going to tell Bax?" Marcie asked.

"Yes. I guess. Sometime," Rena replied. She didn't really know if she would tell Bax or not. It was so hard to predict how he'd react. It might be more trouble than it was worth.

"Now I really need a swim," Julie said. "Anyone coming with me?"

Rena and Marcie begged off. Marcie went back to her room next door.

"You sure you'll be okay?" Julie asked Rena. "I'll stay if you want."

"No. Go. You've been trying to get down there for two hours," Rena told her. "I'm just going to conk out for a while, try to get myself together." She saw that Julie was really concerned. "I'll be fine. Really. Go. Have a good time."

Julie lingered for another moment, trying to decide what to do, then grabbed up her towel and headed out the door.

As soon as she was gone, Rena sank down onto the lower bunk. She knew she wouldn't be able to sleep. She didn't want to sleep. She was afraid of the dreams she might have.

She just wanted to rest. Maybe if she could rest, the sick feeling would go away, the blood would stop pouring, the blood would stop flowing before her eyes, the blood—the blood . . .

No.

She sat up. She couldn't rest.

If she closed her eyes, it would all be there. Present and past.

If she stayed in bed, the blood would drip again.

No. She had to get out of there.

All at once she knew what she had to do.

She had to confront Hedy. She had to tell Hedy that her awful joke would not work. She had to let Hedy know that she would not be frightened away.

The lead role. I have the lead role in a play by a real Broadway director, she suddenly remembered. This is the first good thing to happen to me in three years, and I'm going to hold on to it.

No matter what.

She jumped out of bed and went to the closet. "I'll get changed and go find Hedy and let her know what I think of her and her stupid threats," she told herself.

She felt better already. Taking action made her feel better. She told herself to remember that. Take action, Rena. Don't fall back, don't slip back. Take action. Keep moving. Keep going forward. And maybe, maybe the past will be left behind.

She pulled open the closet, reached in, and began sifting through her clothes.

Wait a minute.

No.

Something's wrong.

Her clothes.

Her clothes.

36

CURTAINS

It took her so long to realize.

The jeans. The tops. Her sweaters. Her sweatshirts. The denim jacket. Her one good dress.

They were all cut up.

Her clothes.

In tatters.

Everything.

All slashed, slashed to pieces.

5

Julie's jeans were a little tight on her, but Rena managed to squeeze into them. Then she found a white midriff top in her dresser drawer that hadn't been slashed.

Hedy had cut only the clothes in the closet. The clothes on the left side of the closet, to be precise. Rena's clothes.

But how did Hedy know which clothes were Rena's and which were Julie's? She couldn't know—could she?

Rena dropped the sandal she was about to put on and stared out the window. She was trying to fight off the thought that had just flashed into her mind, but it had to be confronted.

Was it Julie instead of Hedy?

Did Julie put the swan in the bed and slash Rena's clothes?

Rena tried to remember back to that morning. Yes. Julie had stayed in the room after Rena had gone to the theater. She had showed up about twenty minutes later.

Time enough? Was it time enough to run down to the water, grab a swan, carry it back to the dorm, kill it and plant it in the top bunk, and then slash all of Rena's clothes?

Yes, Rena decided. There probably was time enough.

But why would Julie do it? Julie was her friend, right?

Rena allowed her mind to wander, to follow any path it chose. This was dangerous, she realized. This was something she never did. She always kept her thoughts tightly reined in. She always stayed in control.

But now things were out of control. And she knew she had to figure out why. She had to stop this before—before—

She remembered Julie's expression when she saw the dead swan for the first time. Julie had been as shocked and horrified as Rena. Was that just an act?

Could be. Julie wanted to be an actress, after all.

But why would Julie bring her all the way to a camp in New Hampshire to torture her?

Because of Danny?

No. Julie said she was over Danny, and that she had forgiven Rena.

But was she acting then too?

Was Julie jealous of Rena? Of the way boys were so quickly attracted to her?

No, Rena decided. These thoughts are sick. Julie is my friend. Julie may be dramatic and temperamental, but she isn't vicious.

I just don't want to face the fact that I've made an

enemy, an enemy of someone I don't even know, Rena told herself.

It had to be Hedy.

Hedy had threatened her in front of everyone. Then she had stormed out of rehearsal, determined to carry out her threat.

It had to be Hedy.

Rena slipped the sandals onto her feet. She brushed her hair quickly with four short strokes, rubbed on some clear lip gloss, and headed out into the corridor with determined strides.

She made a face as she stepped over the fake bloodstain George had left on the hall carpet. Hedy's room was just four or five doors down.

What would she say to her? What would she do? Would Hedy deny it? Of course she would.

Then what?

Stay in control, she told herself. Just stay in control.

Breaking into Rena's room and destroying her property was a crime. Killing the swan was probably a crime too. Rena decided she would just tell Hedy that she was going to call the police.

Plain and simple.

If Hedy wanted to deny it, she could deny it to the police.

Then Hedy would know that Rena wasn't going to stand for any more of her cruel pranks.

The idea of the police comforted her for only a few seconds. Then she slipped back into the past, heard once again the wail of sirens and saw the flashing of red lights. Red. Red. Always red. The lights as red as blood.

No. No more police, Rena thought. Please. No more police.

She knocked on Hedy's door, two sharp raps. "Hedy, are you there?" she shouted, feeling strangely excited, as if she were onstage again.

"Hedy! Open up!"

She knocked again, harder this time.

No reply.

She listened for footsteps. Silence.

Then she heard a banging sound inside the room. It was a soft banging. She couldn't figure out what it was. She listened. It repeated. Again.

"Hedy, are you in there?"

She knocked harder.

The only reply was the soft banging sound.

What could it be?

She turned the knob and pushed open the door. "Hedy—anybody here?"

The banging sound came from across the room. It was a yellowed window shade, blown by the wind, hitting against the window.

Hedy has a deluxe room, Rena thought, smiling. We don't have a window shade.

Having solved the mystery of the banging, she turned and started to leave. But she couldn't resist looking around a little more.

The lower bunk was unmade. Hedy's clothes were tossed on it. Rena recognized the flower-patterned wraparound skirt Hedy wore to rehearsals and the green midriff blouse that all the guys thought was so sexy.

I should slash her clothes too, Rena thought. But she quickly fought off the urge, scolding herself.

She walked past the bed to the far wall. The chair was piled with clothes too. Jean cutoffs and a green

Benetton sweater. Did Hedy wear only tops that matched her eyes?

Rena stepped over a rolled-up bikini bottom on the floor to get to the dresser. It was cluttered with makeup jars and tubes, a bottle of spray perfume, combs and brushes, mascara and eye shadow, used Kleenexes smeared with makeup.

She picked up the dangling red plastic earrings that always clattered so loudly whenever Hedy wore them to rehearsal. Rena held them up to her ears and peered into the scratched mirror above the dresser. They seemed so bright against her pale skin and blond hair.

She was still holding the earrings up when she saw the washcloth.

It was balled up on the back corner of the dresser.

Rena stared at it, slowly lowering her hands until the earrings hit the dresser top. She reached out and touched the washcloth.

It was wet.

Cold and wet.

And it was soaked with blood.

Rena stared at it for a long time without moving.

Then, for some reason, she picked it up and unfolded it. It was almost as if she couldn't believe it unless she held it in her hands.

But the washcloth was real. And the blood was real.

So it was Hedy, Rena thought. She tossed the washcloth onto the dresser, knocking over several bottles and jars.

She could feel the anger welling up inside her, anger mixed with disgust.

What right did Hedy have to do those things to her? What right did Hedy have to ruin her summer, to ruin her happiness? What right did Hedy have to spoil everything it had taken her so long to get?

She was still standing at the dresser staring into the mirror when the door opened behind her and Hedy walked in. Rena didn't turn around. She gripped the sides of the dresser and stared at Hedy in the mirror.

Hedy was wearing a black string bikini. She had a white beach towel draped around her shoulders. Her long red hair was tied back in a ponytail.

Hedy's look of surprise quickly gave way to one of suspicion. "What are *you* doing in here?" she asked, staring at Rena's face in the mirror.

Rena turned around slowly to face her.

"Well?" Hedy asked, dramatically tossing the towel on the bed. "What are you doing here?"

"You're not going to scare me away," Rena said in a low voice, pronouncing each word slowly and distinctly.

"But this is my room!" Hedy exclaimed. "You can't come in here!"

"You know what I'm talking about," Rena said, surprised at how calm she was feeling. She was calm, she realized, because she was so clearly in the right.

"No, I do not know what you're talking about. Have you gone bananas or something? I'm going to call Bax. What are you doing with my things? Did you take anything? Why did you come in here, Rena? To steal? What are you doing here?"

Hedy became more frantic as she talked. She pulled open the door and motioned for Rena to leave. "Go on. Get out. Get out now and I won't tell anyone you sneaked in here. Just don't ever try it again."

"No," Rena said. "That isn't going to work, Hedy.

You're not going to turn this around. I know you're the one who killed the swan."

"The what? A swan?" Hedy looked truly confused.

"You're a very good actress," Rena said bitterly.

"I know," Hedy said, her green eyes burning into Rena's. "Better than you'll ever be."

"But you killed the swan. You put it in my bed."

"You're crazy!" Hedy shouted. "You're totally bonkers! Get out! Get out of here! No—wait." She lowered her voice. She gestured frantically for Rena to stay. "I've got a better idea. You stay. I'll go. You stay here and try to get yourself together. Sit down on the bed. Lie down if you want. Just relax. I'll go and get Bax. Don't worry. I'll get help for you."

"Nice try, Hedy. But I'm not the one who needs help. I know you're lying. I know you know what I'm talking about. You can't deny it. You can't pretend I'm crazy. I saw the blood!"

"What? The what?"

Rena grabbed up the washcloth and held it up above her head. "The blood, Hedy. I saw the swan's blood. Here it is. Now tell me I'm crazy."

Hedy started to laugh, a bitter, derisive laugh, which she cut short. "I'm sorry, Rena," she said quietly, "but I still don't know what you're talking about."

"The blood, Hedy. I'm talking about the blood. You slipped up. You forgot to get rid of the evidence."

"Rena, look. I cut my hand this afternoon." Hedy held up her left hand. It was wrapped in a white bandage.

"What?" Rena was still holding the washcloth as she stared at the bandage on Hedy's hand.

"I cut it. I was so angry when I left rehearsal, I

started to run up the hill. I slipped on the tall grass. I cut my hand on a rock."

"Get real, Hedy."

"It's true. I tried to stop the bleeding with that washcloth. But it wouldn't stop. So I went to the dispensary for a bandage."

Rena stared at the bandage. It seemed awfully large for a cut hand.

"I don't believe you, Hedy."

Hedy threw her hands in the air. "I don't care if you believe me or not. It's the truth. Now, put down that stupid washcloth and get out of my room."

"I don't believe you," Rena repeated.

The truth was, she didn't know what to believe now.

"I don't understand this at all," Hedy said, pulling the door open wider, waiting for Rena to leave. "I don't understand why you're trying to spoil my summer. First you take my role from me. Now I find you sneaking around in my room."

"The role is mine!" Rena blurted out. She hadn't meant to say that. She didn't know why she had.

"The role is mine," Hedy corrected her. "You may have it for now. But believe me, Rena, when the last week of camp rolls around, it won't be you up on that stage. It'll be me."

"Don't ever threaten me again!" Rena shouted.

"It wasn't a threat," Hedy said calmly, almost smugly. "It was just a prediction."

Furious beyond words, and frustrated that she wasn't able to get anywhere with Hedy, Rena tossed the washcloth to the floor and strode quickly out of the room. The door was slammed loudly behind her, making her jump.

She stormed out of the dorm and kept going down

the hill toward the water. Anger mixed with confusion in her mind. She really didn't know what to think.

Was Hedy telling the truth? Was the blood on the the washcloth from a cut hand? Or was the bandage a fake?

Hedy had to be the one who killed the swan and cut up my clothes, Rena thought. She's the only one who has threatened me. The only one. And now she's threatened me again.

She really thinks she can take the role away from me. Well, I won't give it up. Not for anything. It's mine. It's something I won. It's something good for me, and I'm going to hold on to it.

She was walking past the theater now, but she didn't see it. A couple of kids smiled at her as they passed, but she didn't see them either.

She didn't see anything. She was too angry to see, too confused.

Was Hedy putting on an act?

She had to be, right? It had to be Hedy. Hedy was trying to frighten her out of camp. Hedy was trying to make her think she was crazy.

It had to be Hedy.

Rena decided. It had to be Hedy.

Just then, a hand shot out and grabbed her shoulder from behind.

6

Rena uttered a loud shriek and spun around.

It was George. He looked as startled as she did. "Sorry, Rena. I didn't mean to scare you."

His dark eyes burned into hers. She tore hers away. She was embarrassed that she had screamed.

"Are you okay?" he asked, sounding genuinely concerned.

"I-I've had a bad day," she told him, forcing a smile, trying to lighten up. "I was thinking of something else. That's why I—that's why you startled me."

"I really didn't mean to—this time." He laughed. "Where are you going?"

"I don't really know," Rena admitted. "Just walking." She nervously raked her hands back through her short hair.

For a brief moment she was tempted to tell George what had happened to her, about the swan, and about her confrontation with Hedy. But she decided against it. She was never comfortable confiding in people, especially in someone she barely knew, someone as strange as George.

"Come sit down and tell me your troubles," George said, pulling her toward a large flat rock beside the path. "I hope you're not still upset by my little performance."

"No," she said, a bit too forcefully. She pulled away from him. "I mean, I don't have time. I can't talk now."

He gave her a hurt-puppy-dog expression. Was he just acting, she wondered, or was he really hurt?

"Come on," he insisted.

He's obviously used to getting his way, Rena thought.

"No. Really," Rena insisted. She turned and headed back up the hill toward the girls' dorm.

The wind blowing down from the top of the hill carried a chill. Clouds rolled over the sun, covering the ground in dark shadows.

He followed her, staying close to her side, his hands in the pockets of his jean cutoffs. "I have a better idea," he said, a sly smile spreading slowly across his face. "Come for a walk later."

"What do you mean? When?"

"You know. After lights-out."

She stopped walking and looked at him. For some reason she laughed.

Again he looked very hurt.

"We could walk down by the water," he said, staring into her eyes. "It's really beautiful then, especially on a clear night. The moon and stars are reflected in the water. It's like a beautiful mirror. The water reflects the sky. The sky reflects the water. It's so amazing, you can get lost in it. You really should see it."

He had moved very close to her. His face was just a few inches from hers, his dark eyes pleading, imploring her to say yes. For a moment she thought he was about to kiss her. She wondered if she would like it. She couldn't decide if she wanted him to or not.

She took a step back.

He talks so beautifully, so romantically, Rena thought. But it's hard to tell what he's really thinking or feeling. It's hard to know what's just a performance and what's him.

"Come on. Come out with me tonight," he urged.

She started to say yes, but something held her back. "Some other time. Maybe," she said, smiling at him apologetically. "I just—it's been such a long, dreadful day. I'm really wrecked. And we have early rehearsals tomorrow."

His dark eyes narrowed and anger flashed briefly across his face. He quickly replaced it with his sorrowful-puppy-dog pout. "Rejection!" he cried dramatically, pretending to stab himself in the heart with an invisible knife.

Rena laughed. "See you at dinner," she said, shaking her head. She hurried up the hill.

This time he didn't follow her.

She turned back once and saw him standing beside the rock, staring up at her, still looking very hurt.

What a character! she told herself. He is cute, though. And interesting. A bit too interesting. You'd better stick to the play, Rena. This isn't the summer for romance. One thing at a time.

As she reached the dorm, she realized that running

into George had cheered her up a bit and made her forget about Hedy for a few minutes. At least *everyone* in this camp doesn't hate me, she told herself.

That night she dreamed about Kenny.

It was her first dream about him since she had arrived at camp.

For the first two years after it happened, she had dreamed about him every night. Then, mercifully, the dreams had diminished to only once or twice a week.

Now it was a month since she had last had the dream. But here it was, back again in all its vivid detail, in all its garish color, in all its screaming horror.

There she was again, wearing those faded red denim jeans and that white sweatshirt, down in the basement of Kenny's house, in the rec room.

The details were all so clear, so vivid. The knotty-pine paneling. The Norman Rockwell calendar with the little boy in the barber chair getting his first haircut. The bamboo fishing poles stacked in the corner, their lines all tangled together. The Ping-Pong table with the torn net, old magazines stacked up on it, *National Geographic*s and *Ladies' Home Journal*s.

She could hear the furnace humming on the other side of the wall. She could hear the washing machine in its rinse cycle. She could hear the *cheep-cheep* of a cricket that had somehow wandered into the basement. So clear. So painfully clear.

And there was Kenny, his hair slicked back, his slender face pale from the bright fluorescent ceiling light.

That look on his face. Playful yet intent. So conspiratorial. Drawing her in, drawing her closer, when all she wanted to do was escape, run away.

Please. Let me out. Don't make me see it all again.

But there she was, back in the basement rec room, back under the pale fluorescent light. And there was Kenny with that weird expression on his face.

And there was the revolver.

"Kenny, what are you doing with that? Put it away."

But he just grinned at her, that sheepish grin, that guilty grin, that grin she'd never seen before, that grin she'd never see again.

"Kenny, please. Put it away."

She watched him drop a single bullet in the chamber. She heard the quiet click it made as the bullet slipped into place. She heard the metallic whir as Kenny spun the cylinder.

Clickclickclickclickclick.

So loud. So clear. So inescapable.

He held the revolver up in front of his face, his slender pale face. He stared at it with his serious dark eyes. He didn't blink. The grin slowly faded.

She saw him lick his lips, his dry, dry lips.

"No, Kenny." Now she was begging. "Don't do it. Please—listen to me. Don't do it."

"Rena, I'm not going to do it," he said, staring at the gun. He handed it to her. "*You're* doing it."

"You're doing it. . . ."

"You're doing it. . . ."

This is where the dream lost its clarity. This is where it all became a blur.

The revolver was in her hand now. Or was it?

She was about to pull the trigger now. Or was she?

Rena tried to see, tried to make the shadows clear. She tried to listen, tried to hear what happened next.

But she was blinded by the glow of the gun. And all she could hear were her own familiar screams.

"No! No! NO!"

She sat up in bed and almost hit her head on the low ceiling. She looked around. She was back in the camp dorm, in the top bunk.

She was back.

She wasn't with Kenny in that basement three years before.

Her heart was pounding. The dream faded slowly.

What was that sound?

Tapping. Tapping. Someone was tapping on the window.

"Julie?" she cried, her voice choked with sleep. Then she remembered that Julie wasn't there. After lights-out, she had sneaked off for a walk with Chip.

The tapping continued, rhythmic, insistent.

Rena climbed down. The floor felt cold against her bare feet. She had no idea what time it was. Julie's bunk was still empty.

It was a clear night. The full moon seemed to be right outside the window, close enough to touch.

Rena looked out. No one there.

She pulled the window up, leaned forward on the sill, and stuck her head out.

No one.

Someone had been tapping. It wasn't part of her dream.

The tall grass beyond the dorm, olive green in the moonlight, bent low, shifting and whispering. The pine trees seemed to shiver as a cool wind slid down from the top of the hill.

No one there.

She closed the window and climbed back up to her bed.

She tried lying on her back, then her side. She couldn't get comfortable, couldn't get sleepy again, couldn't get the dream to go away.

"Kenny, Kenny." She said his name aloud. "If only it were just a dream. If only—"

The tapping started again. Four loud taps, then three quiet taps. Then the pattern repeated.

"I'll ignore it," she told herself. She pulled the pillow over her head, tried to smother out the sound.

Tap-tap-tap-tap. Taptaptap.

She couldn't ignore it.

She threw the pillow to the floor and jumped down after it. Then she pulled up the window and stuck her head out.

"Who's tapping? Who's out there?" she shouted.

Silence.

She saw darting shadows. She heard footsteps behind the trees.

7

Rena stared down glumly at her cereal bowl. "Somebody tell these Rice Krispies to shut up," she muttered. "Why do I have to get a cereal that makes such a racket?"

"Let me guess. You're in a bad mood," Julie said, finishing her orange juice in one long gulp. "Ecch. Pulp." She made a face.

"I'm in a bad mood," Rena repeated lifelessly. "I'm a zombie. That can put a person in a bad mood."

"You look like a zombie. No offense," Julie said. "Didn't you sleep?" She had to shout over the laughter of the kids at the next table. The mess hall was narrow and small, and the low tin ceiling made every sound echo.

"No. No sleep," Rena said, yawning. She picked up a spoonful of cereal, then let it plop back into the bowl. "I can't eat this."

"Are you still upset about—yesterday?" Julie asked, chewing her shredded wheat.

54

"Of course," Rena told her. She wasn't about to say that she'd dreamed about Kenny for the three thousandth time. And she didn't feel like telling Julie about someone trying to drive her crazy by tapping on her window until Julie came back.

Chip smiled at Rena and gave her a friendly wink as he walked past their table, his tray stacked high with about a dozen slices of French toast.

"Good morning, Chip," Julie said, annoyed that he hadn't smiled or winked at her.

"Morning," Chip muttered without looking back.

"Hey, how'd it go with him last night?" Rena whispered, grateful to be able to talk about someone else.

"Oh, wonderful," Julie said sarcastically. She took another spoon of shredded wheat into her mouth and chewed for a while. "He spent the whole night asking me about you. Some date!"

Rena was embarrassed. "Did he really?"

"Yeah. Really. Looks like everyone's interested in you, Rena."

The bitterness in Julie's voice sent a chill down Rena's back. She looked across the table at her friend. Julie kept her eyes down on her cereal bowl.

Julie sounded really jealous of Rena, and she wasn't trying in the slightest to hide it. Was Julie jealous enough to want to get back at Rena? Was she jealous enough to have put the swan in Rena's bed? To have slashed Rena's clothes? To have tapped at the window?

Don't get completely paranoid, Rena silently scolded herself.

Julie was Julie. Julie was always sarcastic. She always said exactly what was on her mind. Rena decided there was no point in trying to turn her only friend at camp into a suspect.

"You haven't touched your breakfast," Julie said. "You'll need some energy for the rehearsal."

"Oh, once I'm onstage, I run on nervous energy," Rena said. She tried to force a laugh, but it didn't quite come off.

"You're so pale," Julie said. She meant it to be sympathetic, but Rena didn't want to hear about how awful she looked.

"Thanks for the clothes," she said, changing the subject. Even though the jeans were a little tight, the yellow T-shirt fitted just fine. "I'm glad you brought so much stuff."

"No problem," Julie said with a mouthful of shredded wheat. "They look better on you anyway."

Again she sounded bitter and jealous.

Again Rena decided to ignore it. She scooted her chair back and stood up quickly. "See you at rehearsal."

Julie glanced up at the Coca-Cola clock over the mess-hall door. "It's early. Where you going?"

"I want to get there early. I decided I'd better tell Bax about some of the things that happened to me yesterday."

Was that a worried look on Julie's face?

Or had Rena just imagined it?

She found Bax in the theater. He was sitting on the edge of the stage, gesturing and talking intently to three kids seated in the front row. They were in charge of building the set. He was dressed in a bright red running suit, which made him look more like Santa Claus than ever. But his impatient manner and torrents of angry words were not at all like those of the jolly old elf.

He was holding up a large sketch and shaking a fist at it. From the back of the theater, Rena could hear only the words *hideous* and *monstrosity*. As she walked closer to the stage, it became extremely clear to her that Bax was not pleased with the set design.

"This isn't fit for graffiti," he was saying as Rena slid into a seat in the fifth row and sank down low, trying to be unobtrusive. "It has to be functional, but it cannot dominate. Do you understand that?"

The three set designers probably didn't have a clue as to what he meant, but they all nodded yes. Bax tore the design in half, then kept tearing the halves until there were several little pieces, which he let drop to the floor. The three kids watched in silence, but Rena could see they were very upset.

"We have all the major elements on stage already," Bax said, pointing to the couch, the sideboard, and the other pieces of furniture and props behind him. "But a bunch of props don't make a living room. I want the audience to know this room, to know this house, to think that maybe they've even been here before. Do you understand? I want you to create a cliché. Think about that."

He paused a few seconds to let them think. Then he climbed to his feet and waved his clipboard, gesturing for them to leave. "I'll meet with you again tomorrow morning before rehearsal. Please come back with a living room and not a train station." He laughed at his little joke, but the three set designers were grim-faced as they stood up and dejectedly headed up the aisle.

He's as mean to them as he is to everyone else, Rena thought.

Bax walked backstage, studying some papers on his clipboard.

Rena jumped up. "Bax!"

He didn't seem to hear her. He kept walking.

"Bax! Can I see you for a minute?"

He stopped and frowned at her. He didn't seem to recognize her. "Just a minute," he said, sounding annoyed.

Rena waited by the front row of seats. A few seconds later he reappeared at the stage door on the left and made his way down the stairs, still studying his papers. Without looking at her, he sat down in one of the front-row seats and began writing quickly.

"I wanted to talk to you," Rena said, standing awkwardly above him. "I've had some—uh—problems."

"Forms, forms," Bax muttered, scribbling furiously.

Rena saw a few kids wander into the back of the auditorium. She realized it must be about time for rehearsal to begin.

"Someone has been trying to scare me, I think," Rena said.

"Ah, these forms. Do you have any idea how many forms a camp director has to fill out?" Bax complained, not lifting his eyes from the papers. "Zoning forms, health forms, tax forms . . ."

More kids wandered in and took seats in the auditorium. A few moved up to the front row. Rena was embarrassed. She really didn't want anyone to hear her telling her problems to Bax. "Someone has been trying to scare me," she repeated, talking quickly in a loud whisper. "Someone slashed my clothes and tapped on my window last night, and—"

"Can this wait? I really don't have time right now," Bax said, still writing.

He hadn't heard a word she'd said.

Rena turned and stomped angrily up the aisle. She was more angry at herself than at Bax. She saw Julie coming down the aisle, but kept going.

"What's wrong? You look upset," Julie said, stopping her with a hand on her shoulder.

"I *knew* it," Rena shouted. "I *knew* he wouldn't listen."

"You told him?"

"I tried to. But he was too busy filling out some stupid forms." She saw Chip and some other guys staring at her, so she lowered her voice. "I knew it. I knew I shouldn't have bothered telling him."

"Guess you were right," Julie said. "Better calm down. Today's got to be a better day, right?"

"Since when are you Miss Cheerful?" Rena asked sarcastically.

"Since you got to be Miss Basket Case," Julie replied.

Rena glared at Julie. She took a deep breath and didn't say anything. Julie's words had really hurt her. I'm not a basket case, she thought. She has no right to call me that. I am a calm, controlled person. I am the most controlled person I know. I am not a basket case.

"Don't look at me like that. I was only joking," Julie said, grinning.

"It wasn't funny," Rena muttered.

"You're just overtired," Julie said. "You need some sleep."

"People! People!" Bax called, standing on the floor in front of the stage, holding up his clipboard. "Please settle down. We have work to do."

The theater quickly became quiet as everyone found a seat.

"Hedy, what are you doing up there?" Bax called up to the stage. He sounded more surprised than annoyed.

Hedy, wearing green short shorts and a tight-fitting green sweater that showed off her ample figure, was standing onstage near the sideboard. She appeared to be fiddling with the props, picking them up and moving them about.

She seemed annoyed by Bax's question. "Bax, you said we'd rehearse my scene first," she said.

"I don't recall that," Bax replied.

"I distinctly remember you telling me," Hedy insisted, tossing her long red hair behind her dramatically. "So I came up here to be ready."

"But I do not wish to rehearse your scene now," Bax said, pronouncing each word separately and distinctly, trying not to lose his temper.

"Well, since I'm already up here . . ." Hedy defiantly sat down on the couch.

"Please," Bax said wearily, his shoulders stooped and his head lowered like an old man's. "Please get down, Hedy. We will rehearse your scene later—if I don't *murder* you first!"

Hedy jumped up off the couch. "You don't have to shout," she said, frowning. She ambled slowly to the side of the stage, taking her time, then exited through the stage door and down the stairs, crossed in front of Bax without looking at him, then started up the aisle.

She stopped next to Rena and gave her a look of exaggerated concern. "Rena, you look terrible!" she cried. "What's wrong? Couldn't you sleep last night? Is the pressure too much for you?"

"Hedy, please find a seat," Bax called, sounding extremely exasperated.

"Was that you tapping on my window last night?" Rena asked her.

Hedy wrinkled her brow. "What? Tapping on your window? What on earth are you talking about?"

"Was it you?" Rena struggled to keep her self-control.

"I was asleep before lights-out," Hedy said. "You can ask Francine, my roommate." She put a hand on Rena's shoulder. "You'd better chill out, kid. You're not gonna make it." She gave Rena a broad, phony smile and continued up the aisle.

"Rena, Chip, let's go," Bax called. "The scene on the couch. From the top. This time, make me believe that you are something more than cardboard cut-outs. Try to work your way up to department-store mannequins."

A few kids laughed at that. Nothing like starting off the day with an insult, Rena thought glumly. She stood up. That heavy feeling in the pit of her stomach, the feeling she got every time she was called to the stage, returned.

Chip was already on the couch when she got up on the stage. She smiled at him, but he looked away. Surprised, she took her place next to him.

"Let's make Bax forget his jokes," Chip whispered, staring down at Bax, who was studying the script. "Let's give him a performance he won't be able to gripe about."

"I'll try," Rena whispered back. Chip seemed so intense, not his usual happy-go-lucky, laid-back self. And he didn't seem the least bit friendly.

What was the matter with him? Rena decided it was

just stage fright. After all, she wasn't the only one who had a right to be nervous, was she?

"Anytime you're ready," Bax called up to them. He took a seat on the aisle and stared up at them, resting his chin in his hand.

"Well, go ahead," Chip snarled impatiently at Rena.

She was so surprised, her opening line went out of her head. She looked at him, puzzled. He was staring straight ahead.

A few seconds later she remembered the line. "Andrea is my friend, my best friend. Did you really think you could come on to her without my knowing anything about it?"

Chip's mouth dropped open and his face filled with surprise. "She told you?"

"Yesss," Rena replied. "She told me."

His face went blank. "So what?"

"So what? So *what?* How long have we been going together? How long?"

"Hold it! Cut! Cut!" Bax yelled. He jumped up from his seat and tossed his clipboard to the floor. "I'm sorry, Rena. I don't believe it."

"What?" Rena could feel her stomach tightening into a hard knot. Her mouth was so dry, she could barely swallow.

"I still don't believe it. You're holding back, Rena. You're holding back too much."

"Well, I was trying—"

"You have to give yourself up, Rena," Bax said. It was one of his favorite lines. They had all heard it at least a hundred times already. "You have to give yourself up to become the character you are playing.

62

Throw away your feelings of embarrassment. Let all your anger out. You have to really hate Chip."

"She's already stabbed me! That's pretty good hate!" Chip cracked.

A lot of kids in the audience laughed, but Bax only frowned. "Let's try again," he said, bending over with great effort to pick up his clipboard.

Rena sat back on the couch and closed her eyes. She realized she was more nervous than ever. How was she going to be good enough to please Bax? He was impossible. He wanted too much from her.

She couldn't let go of herself the way he wanted. She wouldn't. She'd been holding herself in for three years, holding herself back, keeping herself in perfect control. She couldn't just let go now. It would—it would— She was afraid to think of what it might do.

She started the scene again, but her head was spinning with too many thoughts. It wasn't as good as the first time, and she knew it.

"So what? So *what*?" she cried, trying to sound really angry. "How long have we been together—I mean, going together? How long—uh—I'm sorry. I messed up."

Suddenly Chip leapt to his feet and turned to Bax. "This is ridiculous!" he called down angrily. "What is she doing up here?"

Rena couldn't believe her ears. Chip turned back to her. "You're making a fool out of me in front of everyone!" he screamed. "Why are you up here? What do you think you're doing? If you can't get it right, Rena, quit! Do us all a favor and quit!"

8

This is a dream, Rena told herself. A nightmare. Chip isn't standing over me saying these awful things. He wouldn't. He's so funny and easygoing. This has to be a dream.

But even without pinching herself, Rena knew it was no dream. As she stared up at him from the couch, Chip continued his angry outburst.

"Face facts, Rena. You have no talent. Why don't you stop wasting your time? Stop wasting our time too, and give someone good a chance!"

Everyone was staring at her.

Rena had never been so hurt, so humiliated.

Chip glared down at her, red-faced, breathing hard, his boyish looks distorted by anger. He seemed to be waiting for her to say something, challenging her to defend herself.

Chip had no right to talk to her that way. Bax had no right. None of them had a right to scare her, to embarrass her, to hurt her.

Something snapped.

She knew she was out of control.

She didn't care.

She jumped off the couch and shoved Chip back with both hands. "Don't talk to me like that! Don't ever talk to me like that!"

He took a step back, opened his mouth to speak, but no words came out.

"You have no right!" she screamed. "I *do* have talent! I *am* good—as good as you!"

"Hold that! That's perfect!" Bax cried happily, running up to the stage.

Rena stood with her fists clenched, her heart throbbing in her chest. She struggled to catch her breath.

"Rena, I knew you could do it!" With great effort, Bax pulled himself up onto the stage. He climbed to his feet and rushed over to shake her hand. "That's just the anger I want to see. That's just the anger you must convey to the audience. Perfect! Perfect!"

Rena just stared at him. She couldn't talk. She didn't know what to say. She had been out of control, completely out of control. And that frightened her more than anything else that had happened to her that week.

"Do you feel it? Do you feel that true anger?" Bax was asking her, grinning like a tiger after a big steak.

"Yes. I feel it," she said weakly.

"You were good too," Bax told Chip. "Very good performance."

Bax walked off, taking the steps down from the stage.

"I'm sorry. He made me do it," Chip apologized, looking very uncomfortable. "You know that it wasn't me talking. I think you're terrific." He blushed.

"I—I didn't know what to think," Rena admitted.

"You're not still angry, are you?" Chip asked reluctantly.

"Yes. I think I am," Rena said.

"Please—"

"But not at you. At Bax. He really believes he can do anything to us he wants, doesn't he!"

Without thinking, she ran to the steps and caught up with Bax in front of the first row. He turned, surprised. "You're not finished, Rena. Now that you've got it, let's run through it again."

"No. I'm finished," she said angrily, her heart pounding. "Why did you do that to me? Why did you deliberately humiliate me in front of everyone?"

He seemed amused by her question, by her anguish. "Forget the word *me*," he said quietly. "Forget about me, me, me. You are no longer a me. You are the illusion, you are the character you create. You are not Rena. You are not a me. When you are onstage, you are the character you play, the character I wrote."

His speech had had its desired effect. It had calmed her down a little. She was beginning to feel a little more normal, a little less angry, a little more in control.

"You let go for a second, Rena," Bax said, smiling at her. "You let go for a second, and you were wonderful. Now, go back up there and do it again. And again."

"I—I don't know," she said uncertainly. "I don't think I want to."

Bax rolled his eyes, the way he had told her not to. "Why don't you take a short break, then," he said impatiently, scratching his beard. "Have a seat. Catch your breath. Think about your performance."

Rena took the nearest seat and slid down low in it. She wanted to hide inside the chair. She wanted it to curl around her like a closing flower. It felt so good not to have all those eyes staring at her.

Bax's voice interrupted her solitude. "Hedy, why don't you try the scene?" he was saying.

Rena sat straight up. Hedy was bounding eagerly, triumphantly up the steps to the stage. Bax was staring at Rena, enjoying her reaction.

He's doing this just to steam me, Rena thought. He's doing this just to keep me angry, just to make me angry enough to get back up onstage.

Well, it's working.

Bax is truly vicious, she thought. She wondered why Julie couldn't recognize Bax's vicious side, why she always made excuses for Bax.

She turned around in her seat to search for Julie. She saw her in the back of the theater, talking with George.

Meanwhile, Hedy was rolling through Rena's big scene. Naturally she had all the lines memorized. She was tossing her red hair angrily, accusing Chip, threatening Chip with real vehemence.

She's not getting my part, Rena told herself, squeezing her fists tight until her fingernails dug into her palms. She's not getting it. Not getting it.

"Very good, Hedy. Very good indeed," Bax was saying as the scene ended.

Was he saying it because he meant it? Or was he saying it to make Rena mad?

Rena couldn't tell.

Hedy flashed Rena a triumphant smile.

"In fact, that was a little too good," Bax continued.

It was Hedy's turn to look hurt. "What do you mean?" she asked, walking to the edge of the stage, hands on her hips.

"It was slick," Bax said.

"Slick? If you mean professional, I'll take it as a compliment," Hedy said, staring straight at Rena as she said it.

"I didn't say 'professional.' I said 'slick,'" Bax insisted. "I heard words, I saw emotion. But I didn't see them come together in a character."

"Well, let's run through it again," Hedy said, frowning. "I think if I work on it a little more, I'll have it—"

"I'm ready to go back," Rena interrupted.

Bax gave her a pleased smile and gestured with the clipboard for her to resume her place onstage.

"Ba-ax—" Hedy pleaded.

Bax ignored her.

"Bax, my mother has certain expectations, and—"

"Thanks for stepping in," Bax told Hedy coldly. "It's very comforting to know that you're so ready to take over the role should anything happen to Rena."

"But, Bax—"

"Please take your seat, Hedy. We'll rehearse your scene in a little while."

Hedy threw up her hands and stalked off the stage. She stepped past Rena without saying anything. Rena climbed the steps onto the stage.

"Welcome back," Chip said, shaking hands. "Are we friends again?"

"Friends." Rena smiled.

"Let's try the stabbing scene again," Bax called up to them.

"Does she have to stab me? Couldn't we kiss and make up instead?" Chip pleaded half-seriously.

Everyone in the theater laughed.

Bax ignored Chip's suggestion. "I may want to rewrite the action a little," he said, studying the script. "Rena, pay close attention to what you do with the knife. Plunge it in in one motion. It has to look like a sudden, impulsive act of passion. It can't look as if you're thinking about it first."

"Okay. I'll try," Rena said. She walked over to the sideboard and picked up the knife. She gripped it tightly and thrust it forward in a quick stabbing motion.

"Ouch!" Chip cried all the way from across the stage.

A few kids laughed.

"How was that?" Rena asked Bax.

"Better," Bax said. "Try it even faster. Bring your arm back sooner. Then push forward faster. It should look wild and frenzied."

"Wild and frenzied," Rena repeated. She looked at Chip. He had put such an exaggerated frightened look on his face, she had to laugh.

"Okay. Anytime you're ready," Bax said impatiently.

Rena started in the middle of the scene, building her anger, trying to make it real enough for Bax. "So what?" she cried to Chip. "So what? That's all that night was worth to you? A quick so-what?"

"Now, chill out, babes. Let's both just chill out," Chip said, acting appropriately worried.

It's going really well, Rena thought. It feels better this time. It feels right. The anger. I can reach the anger more easily. Bax was right. I guess he knew what he was doing after all.

Rena walked quickly to the sideboard and grabbed

up the knife. She moved quickly. Chip had no chance of getting off the couch.

Remembering Bax's instructions, she pulled her arm back, then thrust forward quickly.

The knife plunged into Chip's side.

He gasped.

His eyes popped open wide. His jaw dropped down and stayed there.

Blood began to spurt around the knife.

He stared up at Rena, disbelief mixed with fear on his face. Real fear. And pain.

"Oh, my Lord!" Rena screamed. "Someone switched knives! It's real! I really stabbed him!"

9

Rena wanted to cry, but the tears wouldn't come.

She lay on her stomach on the lower bunk, staring at the cracks in the white plaster wall, as the stabbing scene replayed itself again and again in her mind.

"First Kenny, now Chip," she muttered. She felt numb. She didn't think she could move, didn't think she'd ever be able to move from that spot or erase the stabbing scene from her memory.

"What? What did you say?" Julie asked. She had brought Rena back to the dorm room. For nearly an hour she had been sitting beside Rena on the bed, trying to offer words of comfort, although she wasn't even sure that Rena knew she was there.

Rena gave no indication of hearing Julie's questions. "More blood, more blood," she muttered.

"What? What are you saying, Rena?" Julie asked, unable to keep the concern out of her voice. "You've got to talk to me. You can't just stare at the wall, talking to yourself."

"More blood," Rena repeated in a whisper.

A loud knock on the door made Julie jump. Lost in her thoughts, watching the stabbing scene re-play itself once again, Rena didn't react at all.

Julie hurried to the door and pulled it open. It was Marcie, looking bedraggled. Her short brown hair was even frizzier than usual, and her eyes were red-rimmed and bloodshot.

"I just came from Bax's office," she said, out of breath. "I thought Rena would want to know that we heard from the hospital in town. Chip's going to be okay."

"That's great news!" Julie cried. She turned back to Rena. "Did you hear that? Chip's going to be okay."

Rena raised herself up and turned around. She didn't seem to understand. Her face registered only confusion.

"The knife went into his side," Marcie said, her high-pitched voice even higher than usual. "It went right between two ribs, but it didn't hit anything vital. He was lucky."

"Yeah, I guess," Julie said.

"How's she doing?" Marcie asked, staring past Julie to Rena.

"Not too well," Julie admitted. "I think she might be in shock. But this news should help snap her out of it."

"The town police are in camp," Marcie told her. "They're fingerprinting everyone. Maybe they can find out who switched the knives on the set. I'd better be going. Tell Rena not to feel bad. Everyone knows it wasn't her fault."

Julie thanked Marcie and closed the door. She was pleased to see that Rena was sitting up now.

"Did you hear that? Chip's going to be okay," she said, walking over and sitting down in the chair across from Rena.

"Good," Rena said. She seemed a little brighter, although she was still as pale as the bedsheets. "First Kenny, then Chip," Rena said, returning to her own world. "What's wrong with me?"

"Everyone knows it wasn't your fault," Julie said.

"Not my fault?"

"Of course not. No one thought for a moment that you wanted to stab Chip."

"Who did it, then?" Rena asked, her eyes focusing on Julie for the first time. "Who switched knives?"

"It had to be Hedy," Julie said matter-of-factly.

"Hedy?"

"Of course. She went up onstage at the beginning of rehearsal, remember? She was fooling around with the stuff on the sideboard. Don't you remember? Bax had to force her off the stage."

"But why?" Rena asked. "Why would Hedy do it? Why would Hedy want to hurt Chip?"

"Chip had nothing to do with it," Julie said. "She wanted to hurt you. She'll do anything to drive you away so she can play the lead."

"But—but I could have killed him!" Rena cried, pulling her hands back through her short blond hair, which was wet and matted together.

"I know," Julie said softly, gazing out the window.

The two girls sat in silence for a while. A little color returned to Rena's cheeks. She began to feel more normal, began to feel some strength returning. "Thanks, Julie," she said softly, breaking the silence.

"Thanks?"

"For being here for me. For taking care of me."

"You're my friend," Julie said, staring out the window.

"I'm a big drag, and I know it," Rena said.

"Who's Kenny?" Julie asked suddenly.

The question surprised Rena. She didn't realize she had mentioned his name to Julie. She considered whether or not to tell Julie the story for a long time. She had never told it to any of her friends in her new life.

"Maybe it's time I told someone," she said finally. "It hasn't been easy keeping it in all these years, keeping everything in."

"If it's too painful . . ." Julie started. She was happy that Rena was coming out of her trance. She didn't want to put her back in it.

"It is too painful," Rena said. "But I want to tell you. Maybe it will help you understand why I reacted the way I did when—when I stabbed Chip, why I went bananas when I found that bloody swan in my bunk."

Julie turned from the window to look at Rena. "I only want you to feel better," she said.

"Kenny—Kenny was my boyfriend back in Hartford," Rena began. She had held the story in for so long, the words tumbled out now. "That's where I lived before I moved to Cambridge, before I met you. Kenny was great. I mean, I really loved him.

"I guess he was always a little crazy. He was always doing crazy things, saying things. Well—you could never predict what he was going to say or do. And you could never predict what kind of mood he'd be in. He was very moody. I mean with a capital *M*. Sometimes he'd be so happy and so much fun. And other times, he'd be so low I couldn't even talk to him. He'd get down on himself and talk about how worthless he was. Stuff like that.

"He lived with his mother in Hartford. They had a small house, nothing fancy. They didn't have a whole lot of money. In fact, they were quite poor. His parents were divorced when Kenny was ten. His brother and sister lived in California with Kenny's father.

"That bothered Kenny a lot. He and his brother had been very close. He missed his brother all the time. He had a lot of guilt feelings, you know, how sometimes kids whose parents get divorced take some of the guilt on themselves."

"I guess," Julie said. "I've never really had to think about it."

"Well, Kenny had a lot of problems, mind problems I guess you'd call them," Rena continued, her face blank, expressionless, sitting very still with her hands clasped tight together in her lap. "But even so, he could always make me laugh. I guess I loved him for that."

She paused for a while. Julie shifted uneasily in the chair, bringing her legs up until she could rest her chin on her knees.

"I don't think Kenny ever believed anyone could really love him." Rena's voice broke as she started her story again. "He just never got used to his family being split up like that. He never got used to not having his little brother around, having his father so far away. I think he really felt abandoned.

"He got more and more depressed. It was terrible. I tried to help him be happy, tried to joke him out of it, tried to make him feel loved. But he was out somewhere where I couldn't reach him. Know what I mean?"

"I guess," Julie said.

"He was with me, but he was also somewhere else, somewhere alone. And it wasn't a good place. I—I felt so helpless. I just couldn't get to him at all. And all I could do was watch him grow more and more unhappy, with his life, with himself. He seemed desperate to do something, but he didn't know what.

"Then one night we were in the rec room down in his basement. He had a gun, a revolver. I don't know where he got it. I don't know why I didn't grab it away the moment I saw it.

"I was so frightened. I don't think—I don't think—I don't remember what I was thinking. Kenny put one bullet in the gun. Then he handed it to me. He told me to spin the cylinder. I didn't want to. I didn't want to touch the gun at all. But he made me.

"I don't remember spinning the cylinder. I don't really remember holding the gun. I just remember the gun going off. I'll never forget the sound. I'll never forget the blood."

"Rena, stop—" Julie cried. "This is too painful for you. Don't—"

Rena didn't seem to hear Julie. She kept right on with her story. "There was blood everywhere. Just blood. That's all that was left of Kenny. That's all I remember. I don't know whether I shot him or whether he shot himself. I can't make it come clear.

"I see it all the time. For two years I saw it every night of my life, in every dream I had. But I can't make it come clear. I can't remember what really happened."

"How awful," Julie whispered. "Rena, I had no idea."

"It was in all the Connecticut papers. Front page," Rena continued. "The police said I didn't do it. They called it an accidental suicide. An accidental suicide. But a lot of people believed that I killed Kenny. A lot of people. I was one of them. For a long time I really believed that I did it. Now I don't know. I don't know what to think. I just don't remember.

"My family and I, we had to move, of course. There was no way we could stay in Hartford after that. No way I could face my friends, Kenny's friends, Kenny's mother.

"We moved to Cambridge. A little less than three years ago. Remember? That's when I met you. My first day at school. You were my first new friend, my first new friend in my new life. Only I couldn't leave my old life behind.

"My life was a nightmare. People say that a lot in movies, in books. But for me it was true. It was the same nightmare, over and over. I couldn't get away from it, couldn't leave it behind.

"Getting the lead in *Curtains* was the best thing that's happened to me in three years. That's why the role means so much to me. It's the first sign I've had that I can be something, that I can do something, that I'm a good person."

Rena lay back on the bed and pulled the pillow down over her face. She had never told her story to anyone. Now she had. She thought she might feel different now, feel lighter maybe. But she felt the same. She picked up the pillow and tossed it aside.

"Wow," Julie said after a long while. "Wow. Rena,

I'm so sorry—" She stared out the window. She was having difficulty looking at Rena. "Now I understand why you're so insecure. Now I understand why you have to have all the boys."

Rena felt as if she'd just been stabbed with the knife.

Had Julie really said that to her? Was that Julie's true response to her horrifying story? So unsympathetic? So uncaring? So bitter?

"Now I understand why you have to have all the boys."

Rena turned her head away and stared at the wall. She suddenly realized that she had told her story to the wrong person.

Julie wasn't her friend after all.

No real friend would react that way.

Julie must still be angry about Danny.

Deep down, Julie must hate Rena.

But did she hate her enough to bring Rena to this camp just to torture her?

10

"You never knew the victim before arriving in camp?"

"That's right."

The young police officer frowned and looked down at his small notepad, trying to think of his next question.

"Do you have to call him a victim?" Julie piped in. She and Rena were seated in a corner of the mess hall.

The police officer, Lieutenant Byron Charnick it said on a metal tag above his shirt pocket, stood uncomfortably in front of them, shifting from foot to foot, intensely studying his notes between every question. "Maybe he was an attempted murder victim. Maybe he was an accident victim," he said, tightening his lips beneath his sparse black mustache. "But he was a victim nonetheless."

Lieutenant Charnick had been questioning Rena and Julie for about half an hour. He told them when they first met him that the only fingerprints found on the knife were Rena's. The collapsible knife had been found on the stage floor beside the couch. It had no fingerprints on it at all.

"Do you know of anyone who might have a motive for killing the vic—the young man?" Charnick seemed pleased by his own question. He didn't get too many stabbing cases in this tiny rural precinct of New Hampshire.

"No," Rena said softly. She'd been answering all of his questions with one- or two-word answers. So far, she'd done an excellent job of keeping herself in control. She hadn't slept at all the night before, which was making her more edgy, more alert, better able to answer the young cop's questions.

If only he'd go away, she thought. He isn't going to accomplish anything here. He isn't going to help anyone.

"Did you talk to Hedy?" Julie suddenly asked, shooting a glance at Rena. "She was onstage before the rehearsal."

"Which one is she?" Charnick shuffled through his notes, squinting at them for some reason. "The redheaded girl?"

"Yes. That's Hedy," Julie said, trying to read his notepad upside down.

"Yeah, I talked to her. Her prints were on the side table. But not on the knife. Is there something you want to tell me about her? Does she have a motive for wanting to harm this boy?"

Julie started to say something, but Rena interrupted. "No. No, she doesn't. We just saw her up on the stage, that's all."

"A lot of people were on the stage," Charnick said, closing his little notebook and tucking it into his shirt pocket. He narrowed his eyes and looked Rena up and down. "You look pretty tired," he said.

"I am," Rena said. "I'm pretty upset and exhausted."

"First time you stabbed someone, huh?" Charnick said, and then laughed. He stopped when he saw Rena's face. "Hey, you can relax," he said. "It looks like an accident to me. That's what my report is gonna say." He kicked an empty paper cup across the floor. "Thanks for your help. Get some sleep, ya hear?" He turned and clomped noisily out of the mess hall.

"An accident! It was no accident!" Julie proclaimed when he was out of sight.

"We don't know that," Rena said wearily.

"We know that Hedy switched knives," Julie insisted.

"No, we don't. We don't know anything," Rena said. She got up and started toward the door.

"Where you off to? Bed?" Julie called after her.

"I'm going for a quick walk," Rena said. "Clear my head." She walked to the mess-hall door, then turned back to look at Julie. To her surprise, Julie seemed lost in thought, and she had the strangest frown on her face.

The next night Rena had trouble falling asleep again. Her mind just refused to turn off. She had spoken to Chip on the phone that afternoon. He sounded good. And he certainly didn't hold her responsible for what had happened.

That made her feel better. And having had a day to herself, a day when she didn't have to rehearse, didn't have to face Bax and his unending demands, made her feel better too.

So why couldn't she get to sleep?

It was silent in the girls' dorm, hours after lights-out. Julie had sneaked out with another boy, one of the set designers.

Rena closed her eyes tight and tried picturing sheep, then fluffy gray clouds floating over a meadow.

She was just starting to drift off when the tapping sounds started again. The same rhythmic, insistent tapping.

She tried to ignore it. She pulled the pillow over her head. But the tapping was loud enough to hear through the pillow.

She sat up. More tapping. I can't let this happen to me, she thought. This is the summer I've been waiting for, the summer I can remake my life.

The tapping continued.

She jumped up, pulled up the window to open it, stuck her head out, and shouted, "Stop it! Hedy, leave me alone! Stop it!"

George jumped back from the wall in surprise, tumbled over a tree stump, and went sprawling onto his back.

"Oh!" It was Rena's turn to be surprised. "What are you doing out there? I thought—"

George groaned and pulled himself up. "I've had warmer greetings," he said, brushing off his jacket.

"What are you doing out there?" Rena repeated.

"I wondered if you wanted to come out and play." He gave her his best Matt Dillon smile.

"No," she said. "Go away. I just want to sleep. I—"

"Come on out for a walk," he urged softly. "A short walk. It's a beautiful night."

She looked up at the clear, starry sky. The full moon

seemed close enough to touch. "I don't know, George . . ."

"Come on," he said, stepping up so close to the window they were practically nose to nose. "I won't bite. Much."

She laughed. "It's kinda windy."

"But the air is warm," he said. "Come on out, Rena. There won't be another night this beautiful for at least a trillion years."

"Okay," she said, surprising herself. Then she changed her mind. Then she changed her mind again.

She went over to the bed in the dark, pulled off her nightshirt, and fumbled around in the dresser until she found a T-shirt and a pair of Julie's shorts. Why am I doing this? she asked herself as she slipped into her sandals. "Why not?" she answered herself aloud.

Back at the window, she boosted herself up to sit on the ledge and stuck out her hands. George reached under her arms and helped her down to the ground. He was stronger than he looked, she realized.

Clouds had covered the moon, shutting off the only light. "It's so dark, I really can't see who you are," she said softly, feeling excited and kind of floaty.

"I'm the Mysterious Stranger," George said in a deep voice that sounded more comical than mysterious. "I come only at night to tap on girls' windows and steal them away."

"Cute," she said, returning to earth. "Very cute. I must be out of my mind to go out with you on a night with a full moon."

He reared his head back and howled at the top of his lungs.

"Is that a werewolf or an unhappy puppy dog?" She laughed.

"I'm not sure," he said, turning serious quickly.

They walked through the tall grass, cold and wet from the night dew. Rena couldn't see the line of tall pine trees, but she knew they were there. Fireflies darted and dived between their low branches, providing the only light.

"Why don't we roll down the hill?" George suggested.

"No way," Rena said. "We'd be soaked by the time we reached the bottom."

"But it would be exciting," he persisted.

"I've had enough excitement this week," she said wearily.

"But it would be dangerous," he said, making the word *dangerous* seem even more dangerous. "Don't you ever choose to be dangerous?"

"I came out with you!" Rena replied. "That's dangerous enough. I don't have to roll down the hill too, do I?"

He didn't reply.

As they made their way down the hill toward the water, the clouds parted, leaving a bright full moon in their wake. The sky brightened, illuminating the grass beneath their feet. The pine trees came into view. Rena saw two baby rabbits hop under a low shrub.

She shivered.

"Hey, you're cold," he said. "Here. Take this." He pulled off his jacket and handed it to her.

"Thanks," she said, smiling. "These aren't your initials. Who's A.M.?"

The question seemed to startle him. He thought for a moment before replying. "I borrowed the jacket. It's not mine. It belongs to a guy I know named Andy."

She pulled the jacket around her shoulders. He

walked on ahead. "Wait up. What's your hurry?" she called.

"No hurry," he said with a shrug. "I just like to get where I'm going." His mood had changed. He was no longer playful. He had become almost glum.

"I enjoyed the day off," Rena said, trying to get some kind of conversation started. "It was nice not having Bax yell at me for a day."

"You don't like him, huh?" It sounded like an accusation.

"No. Not much," she replied honestly.

"He's not a bad guy. He gave me a scholarship to camp," George said. "He knows about my family. We're—uh—poor." He laughed, a short, bitter laugh. "*Poor* isn't the word. What's the word just below *poor* when you're too poor to be poor?"

"I don't know." The question caught Rena off-guard. She had come out for a romantic walk. Why had George's mood turned so grim?

"Well, I can tell you a lot about being poor even if I don't know the word for it. Want to hear?" It was more of a threat than a question.

Rena stopped walking. George was staring into her eyes, that same intense stare that had frightened her the last time she talked with him.

I should have stayed in the dorm, she told herself. He's so strange, always on edge, always ready to explode. Why do I have the feeling he's just about to do something really awful?

She suddenly felt silly. He was a theater person. He just had an intense way of expressing himself, that was all. He wasn't really dangerous. He was actually very sensitive, and kind of nice.

They sat down on the ground a few yards from the

water. The tide was out, and low waves lapped quietly against the shore, the water sparkling magically under the moonlight. On the dock to their right the old boathouse stood in shadows, creaking as the water moved in and out.

She pulled his jacket around her tighter. He put his arm around her shoulder. He pulled her close, turned her face to his, and began to kiss her.

Well, he said he likes to get where he's going, she told herself, kissing him back, bringing her hand gently up to his cheek.

She tried to end the kiss, but he pressed his mouth tighter against hers.

She tried to back away, but he had his arms around her now and was pulling her closer.

His kiss became harder, harder. His teeth were pushing against her lips. He was hurting her. It was more like an attack than a kiss.

"No!" she cried out, and struggled to get out of his grasp. She jumped to her feet. "George—"

He grabbed both of her arms and pulled her back down roughly. He moved forward to kiss her again.

She tried to pull away. But he was very strong.

"George, please— Let go of me!"

Startled by Rena's outcry, George let go. His look of surprise quickly turned to one of complete bewilderment. "Hey, what's wrong?"

Rena rubbed her arms and shoulders. George had gripped them so tightly, they ached. "What's wrong? What's wrong with *you?*" she demanded, still out of breath, her heart pounding.

"Sorry," he said quietly. "I really am sorry, Rena." He jumped up and tenderly put a hand on her shoulder.

She backed away. "Don't touch me."

"I really didn't mean anything," he said, his dark eyes seeking hers. "I—I guess I'm like most actors. I can't stand rejection."

She turned away from him. Her lower lip was bleeding from his kiss. "You frightened me. You were like an animal."

"I didn't mean to be. Please. Believe me. You've got to accept my apology. It'll never happen again."

"No, it won't," she said angrily. She pulled off his jacket and tossed it at him without meeting his eyes. Then she started running up the hill. The cool night air felt good on her arms. She suddenly wanted to run, and keep running forever.

"Wait!" he called, taking off after her. "At least let me walk you back."

She didn't slow her pace, but he quickly caught up with her. "Please. Let me. You've got to accept my apology, Rena. You've got to. I feel terrible."

"Apology accepted," she said coldly, and kept running up the hill through the tall, wet grass.

He stopped. She looked back a few seconds later to see him standing still in the moonlight, his eyes on her, a twisted frown on his face. A frown of disappointment? Of regret? Of anger?

Rena couldn't tell.

And she didn't want to think about it.

She had made a mistake. She should never have sneaked out with George. She should never have let him tempt her. She knew he was too intense, too strange, too needy.

George wasn't what she needed. Not now. Not ever.

What she needed, Rena thought as she reached the low dormitory and climbed back into her dark room through the open window, what she needed was a good night's sleep.

She stared out into the night. Had George followed her? No. No one was out there. The moon had disappeared behind a thick curtain of clouds. And then it started to rain, large, round drops falling slowly at first. In seconds it became a downpour.

She closed the window. Shivering from the cold, her arms covered in goose bumps and aching from

George's grasp, she undressed quickly and felt blindly through her trunk until she found the flannel nightshirt she had brought.

Julie still hadn't returned. She was probably caught in the downpour with the boy she had sneaked out to meet. The rain pummeled the flat roof of the dorm, creating a deafening, steady roar. Rena hoped that Julie was able to find shelter somewhere out of the storm.

She climbed up to the top bunk and slipped into bed, pulling the sheet and wool blanket up to her chin. After a short while she began to feel warmer.

Sleep, sleep. Go to sleep. She tried repeating the words in her mind, but it didn't help. She was wide-awake.

The scene with George down by the water kept replaying itself in her mind. Again George pulled her close and began to kiss her. She tried to pull away, to escape from his grip. Pleasure turned to pain. Anticipation turned to fear.

She couldn't get over her shock at George's sudden violence. His kiss—it didn't seem like a way of expressing affection or warm feeling. The kiss was hostile. No. More than that. It seemed to be filled with hatred.

Or was she making too much of it?

George was an emotional guy, after all. Maybe he just got carried away.

He certainly was apologetic afterward. He seemed upset and terribly sorry about acting so strangely.

Maybe he really did care about her.

No one had really cared about her that way for three years. She hadn't allowed anyone to get really close to her.

Sleep. Sleep. Go to sleep.

She wasn't going to allow George to get close either.

She decided she'd try to avoid him for the rest of camp. She'd be polite. She wouldn't be cold to him.

But no more walks after lights-out. No more heart-to-heart talks. No more kisses.

She could feel herself getting sleepy, feel herself begin to drift off. She felt her lip. It was definitely cut. George had cut it with his teeth.

Sleep. Sleep. Go to sleep. It was warm now. Warm and cozy. The rain had slowed to a gentle hissing whisper above her on the dorm roof.

Quiet. It was getting so quiet.

And then she heard the tapping sound on the window.

No, she thought. Please, no.

But the tapping repeated, louder, more insistent. Three loud taps followed by four quiet taps.

Please, no.

Wearily she pushed down the bedcovers and climbed down to the floor.

Tap-tap-tap. Taptaptaptap.

Feeling the anger build quickly, she pulled the window up with a hard tug.

"Bax! What are *you* doing out there?"

He grinned at her. The rain had slowed to a drizzle. His white beard and eyebrows were glistening from the raindrops they had trapped. He was wearing a white crew-neck sweater and white sailor pants. The rain and the mist, illuminated by pale moonlight, surrounded him, giving him an unreal quality, as if he were some sort of glowing white spirit.

"Bax, what do you want?"

"We need to be spontaneous sometimes," he said mysteriously, almost shyly.

"What? It's raining."

She suddenly felt foolish. He was wet enough to know that it was raining.

"Step outside," he said. It sounded more like an order than a request.

"What? I can't. I'm not dressed. I'm in a nightshirt. It's so late, Bax. What do you want?"

He stared at her. He seemed to have a ring of white light all around him. He looked like a big light bulb, all white and shiny. A furry white light bulb, Rena thought, smiling despite her bewilderment at what he was doing outside her window.

"Step outside," he repeated. "I want to run through the stabbing scene with you."

A chill ran down Rena's back. Why did Bax suddenly look so ominous, so threatening?

"I can't," she insisted. "It's raining, Bax. And it's so late."

"Come on, Rena," Bax said, frowning impatiently, the white glow around him brightening. "Come out. I want to practice the scene now. I think we need to."

"Bax, you're frightening me," she admitted. "We can't practice the scene. Chip isn't here. He's in the hospital—remember?"

"That's okay. I have a replacement," Bax said in a tone that sounded positively threatening.

"A replacement? Who?"

As Rena peered into the darkness, Kenny stepped into view, eerily illuminated by Bax's white glow.

Bax's eyes glowed bright yellow and he gave her an evil, leering grin. He pushed Kenny up to the window. "Here, Rena. Stab him. Stab him!" Bax cried.

"No!" Rena screamed. *"No!"*

She awoke and sat straight up in bed, hitting her head on the low ceiling.

What an awful nightmare.

Her head ached. The rain was still pounding the roof.

She glanced down to the window to reassure herself that it was still closed, that it had all been only a nightmare.

"Which is the worse nightmare?" she asked herself. "When I'm asleep, or when I'm awake?"

12

The next morning began for Rena with an argument with Julie.

Rena couldn't quite figure out what the argument was about, why it had started, or why Julie chose to continue it. It had something to do with a pair of Julie's jeans that Rena had worn and had returned to the wrong dresser drawer.

"Julie, I'm sorry. I didn't know you had any kind of a system," Rena said, standing on Julie's bed to make her own.

"Oh, I see. I get it. You just think I'm a total slob," Julie snapped.

"That's not what I said," Rena insisted. She climbed down and faced her friend. She felt uncomfortable since she was dressed from head to foot in another outfit of Julie's.

"That's what you implied," Julie said, carefully folding the jeans in question. "I don't mind lending you my clothes, Rena, but—"

"But I guess you do mind," Rena said, sounding hurt. "Otherwise I can't imagine why you'd be carrying on like this."

"It's just the principle," Julie said.

"What principle?"

Julie didn't reply. She jammed the jeans into her bottom dresser drawer. "Wow. Kevin and I got drenched last night. One minute it was a beautiful night. The next minute it was Noah's ark time."

"What did you do?" Rena asked, still feeling hurt but delighted to be able to change the subject.

"We ran into the old boathouse. The roof leaked, but it was better than being outside. Kinda romantic, actually." She gave Rena a sly smile. She seemed to be over her momentary anger.

I wonder what's really troubling her, Rena asked herself. It isn't like Julie to make a fuss about where jeans are put away. She *is* a slob!

"Rena, how come you still look so tired?" Julie asked, suddenly concerned.

"Because I'm tired, I guess." Rena shrugged. "I haven't been sleeping well." She looked out the window. The sun was shining bright and golden over the tall pine trees. "I haven't been sleeping at all, actually."

"I can see that," Julie said, studying her. "You look wasted."

"Thanks a lot," Rena said, annoyed. "You sound just like Hedy. Next you'll be telling me I look too awful to go onstage."

"Rena, stop saying things like that. I'm your friend, remember? And as your friend, I'll say this—and I really mean it as a friend—if being in the play is making you so nervous you can't sleep, you really *should* quit. It isn't worth losing your health over."

"Thanks a bunch for the support," Rena said coldly. "You know it isn't the play that's got me upset, Julie. It's everything else that's been happening to me here."

Julie started to reply, but she was interrupted by a knock on the door. "Who is it?" she called.

"George."

Julie gave Rena a bewildered look. "What does he want?" she whispered.

Rena didn't feel like telling Julie about the night before. She didn't feel she could confide in Julie anymore. "I'm dressed. I'll go see," she said.

She walked over to the door and pulled it open halfway. "Good morning, George," she said flatly, without any emotion at all.

He gave her his best Matt Dillon smile, then looked disappointed when she didn't respond to it. "Good morning, Rena," he repeated, almost shyly. "How are you this morning?"

"Fine. Okay. Well, actually, I didn't sleep too well last night."

He looked concerned. "Oh. I—uh—not because of me, I hope."

"No. Not because of you."

He stared at her for a long time without saying anything.

"What do you want, George?" she asked impatiently. "It's early. We're still getting dressed."

"Sorry. I just—uh— Well, I ran into Bax this morning, and he's sick."

"What?" Julie popped her head out. "Bax is sick?"

She pulled open the door. A couple of girls from other rooms came out into the dark, narrow hall.

"Yeah. Well, he just said he wasn't feeling tip-top. Something he ate or something. He said there won't be rehearsal until tonight." George smiled at Rena. "Guess that means we have a free day."

Rena backed up into the room. George followed her in. Julie gave her a surprised look, then headed out to join the other girls on their way to the mess hall.

"So, how about it?" George asked when everyone had gone and the dorm was quiet.

"How about what?" Rena asked, annoyed. What was he doing in here when she had already decided not to have any more to do with him? Why was he staring at her so confidently now? Why was he grinning like that? Did he know something she didn't?

He looked as if he had something to tell her, something he could hardly keep in another second.

"What is it, George?" she asked warily, pulling her hands back through her hair, then crossing her arms in front of her.

"I just thought since we were going to be costars in the play, maybe we could spend the day together. Go for a swim, maybe. Do a little rehearsing."

"Costars? Are you for real? What are you talking about?" He had just told her his big news, and her only reaction was to get annoyed. It wasn't nice. She wasn't being fair to him. But she realized she didn't care.

"That's how I happened to see Bax this morning," George explained, dropping down onto Julie's bed and stretching out on his back, putting his hands behind his head. "Bax called me into his office first thing. He said Chip was doing okay. But when he gets out of the hospital, he's going home. He isn't coming back to camp. So Bax gave me his role."

"You?"

"Don't look so shocked. Maybe I'm a real talented guy."

"But—"

"So how about it?"

Rena didn't say anything.

"How about a swim after breakfast?"

"No," she told him, keeping her arms crossed, a protective shield in front of her. "I mean, no thanks."

He sat up, a hurt expression on his face. "Why not?"

"I'm too tired. If we have the whole day off, I'm going to use it to rest up."

"Well, come rest with me." He seemed really desperate for her to say yes. She walked over to the dresser so she wouldn't have to meet his pleading eyes.

"No. I can't, George. Some other time. Maybe."

"You're still bent out of shape about last night, aren't you?" His tone was more accusing than apologetic. It made Rena even more determined not to spend time with him.

"I want to memorize my lines, and take a long nap."

"We're going to be acting together. We should memorize our lines together. We can go down to the dock and—"

"No, George. Please." She walked over to the door and opened it wide, an unsubtle hint for him to leave. "I can't memorize lines that way. I have to be by myself."

He looked as if he'd just been mortally wounded. He pulled himself up slowly from the bed and sighed. "Listen, Rena, if you change your mind . . ."

"See you tonight at the rehearsal," she said.

She gave him a little wave as he walked past her into the hallway. "And stop looking as if someone has just killed your puppy," she called after him.

She meant it to sound light. But he didn't turn around or react in any way. When he turned the corner and disappeared from view, she closed the door, breathed a long sigh of relief, and climbed back into bed.

Bax didn't look well. His Santa Claus cheeks, normally so rosy, looked pale, his whole face was drawn and lifeless. His gray running suit was wrinkled and had dark brown food stains across the front of the sweatshirt. One of his white high-tops was untied.

He sat quietly on the edge of the stage, studying his clipboard as everyone wandered into the theater for the evening rehearsal. Occasionally he glanced up to frown at them in greeting.

Rena felt rested and a little better prepared to face Bax and the world. She had used the day to nap and to study her lines, just as she had told George. An express package from home had brought her a new shipment of clothing. Being able to wear her own jeans and sweater made her feel more comfortable too.

So when Hedy began the evening by insulting Rena at the entrance to the theater, Rena took it in stride and didn't react with shock, or anger, or embarrassment the way Hedy would have liked.

"Let me get the door for you. You look so exhausted," Hedy had said, stepping past Rena to pull open the heavy wooden door to the theater.

"Thanks," Rena said, walking quickly through the open door without a glance at Hedy.

Hedy followed close behind, determined to rile Rena. "At this rate, you'll never make it to opening night. Why not save yourself a lot of anxiety and unhappiness and let me take over the role now?"

Rena spun around. "Hedy, all the tricks in the world won't get me to give up this role."

"Tricks? What tricks?" Hedy couldn't hide the fact that she was pleased she was able to get a reaction from Rena.

"You and I both know what I'm talking about," Rena said, her voice calm and controlled.

"You're losing it, Rena," Hedy said quietly, shaking her head in mock sadness. "You're really losing it. You need a long rest somewhere far away."

Rena turned without replying and headed down the aisle.

"I don't need tricks to get that role. I have talent!" Hedy called after her.

Rena ignored her and took a seat in the second row. I'm not going to let her see me as vulnerable again, Rena thought. I can be as strong as she is. Even stronger.

Even though it was the middle of summer, the theater was cold and damp. Rena began to get a nervous feeling in the pit of her stomach. She knew she'd be up on the stage soon, having to prove herself again and again, having to show Hedy, and Bax, and all the rest of them that she deserved to have the lead in the play.

After a while Bax struggled to his feet and raised his clipboard above his head for silence. "People, people," he called out. His voice sounded weak. His words didn't echo off the high rafters the way they usually did. "Sorry to interrupt your summer fun for a little theater work."

The auditorium quickly grew silent. Bax was speaking so quietly, everyone had to strain to hear what he was saying.

He doesn't really look sick, Rena thought. He seems completely bummed out, completely dispirited.

"I regret to say that I am feeling more than a little bit like King Lear this evening," Bax said wearily, not even bothering to do his usual pacing back and forth across the stage. "I'm feeling ready to give away my kingdom. The only problem is, of course, that I do not possess a kingdom. So I suppose we shall have to proceed with our work here."

He paused for a long while, staring straight ahead toward the back of the small theater. The clipboard slipped out of his hand and clattered to the floor of the stage. He didn't bother to retrieve it.

"Before we return to our scenes in *Curtains*, I want to talk a little bit about fear," Bax said, trying unsuccessfully to clear his throat as he talked. "*Curtains*, as you may have figured out by now, is about fear. It's about different kinds of fear, actually. The fear of losing control. The fear of the consequences of losing control. The fear of dying suddenly, of being murdered by someone who has lost control.

"*Curtains* is about fear. And I believe the theater itself is about fear. I know that I personally have been largely motivated by fear. Fear of not getting backers for a show. Fear of failure. Of embarrassment. Fear of bad reviews.

"I confess to you that I use fear when working with you, when trying to mold you into actors and actresses

100

fit to perform in front of the most discerning audience. Fear of ridicule. Fear of my disapproval. Fear of appearing foolish in front of your peers. I use all of these fears in motivating you to find your character, to find your talent, and to do your best work.

"Tonight I'm asking you to find the fear within yourselves, to find the fear you need to perform your role to the very utmost of your ability. We all have fear within us," he said, stepping so close to the lip of the stage that the toes of his sneakers protruded over the edge. "The question is, how do we locate the fear? How do we bring it forward? How do we use it?"

Bax's lecture seemed to exhaust him. His shoulders slumped forward and he sighed. He pulled out a large blue polka-dot handkerchief and mopped his forehead.

What a strange speech, Rena thought, checking to see if the other cast members felt as uncomfortable as she did. Why does he think he has to use fear to motivate us? Why not use encouragement, enthusiasm, support?

There's enough fear in just getting up on the stage, she thought. Wouldn't everyone give a better performance, wouldn't I give a better performance, if he showed me how to lessen the fear instead of increasing it?

She didn't have time to think about it any longer. Bax called George and her to the stage to run through the stabbing scene.

Rena had entered the theater feeling rested, more fit, and ready to face the challenges that awaited her onstage. But after Hedy's renewed attacks and Bax's lecture, she was beginning to regret leaving her dorm room.

All of her doubts and inhibitions came back. And seeing the knife on the table, the knife she would have to pick up and use again, plunged her back to the whole horrible scene with Chip, plunged her back, back to one scene of blood and then another, and she was overcome with dread. All of her good feelings, all of her renewed strength, abandoned her as she stepped onto the stage and faced a smiling George.

She felt like an observer as she ran through the scene. It was as if she were in the auditorium watching from the third row, watching someone else speak the lines and go through the motions that ended in the collapsible knife sliding between George's ribs.

Was she performing well? Was she finding the fear Bax had requested? Was she getting across the intensity, the fury of a person so out of control as to be able to thrust a knife into another person?

She couldn't tell.

She was just going through it, playing a part, unable to concentrate, unable to clear her mind enough to let the character take over.

"Stop. Please stop," Bax said sorrowfully. "I can't bear this any longer."

What? What was he saying? Rena held the knife in her hand, gripping it so tightly it hurt. Was he stopping the scene? Was he about to criticize her again, to scream at her, to try to make her even more fearful than she already was?

"I can't do this anymore," Bax cried, his voice weak and tired. He heaved the clipboard across the stage. It hit the curtain and slid down to the floor.

"I'm wasting my life on amateurs, amateurs with no desire," he complained to no one in particular, to everyone. "I'm wasting my energy, my being, my talents, my life. I can't! I'm sorry, but I just can't put myself through this charade any longer."

Suddenly all of the lights in the theater went out.

A few kids cried out in surprise. Then there was silence.

Rena sat down on the couch on the stage. Where was George? She didn't know.

"Bax, what happened? Is it a fuse?" a boy called out.

Bax didn't reply.

Rena heard a scraping sound, like a chair being dragged across the stage. She heard footsteps, shuffling noises.

"Is anyone going to do anything?" she heard Hedy shout from the back of the theater.

"Bax, is it a power failure?" another girl asked.

"Bax?"

No reply.

"Let's not panic, everyone," George said suddenly. He was somewhere across the stage from Rena. "If the lights don't come back on, we can easily make our way out of the theater."

"Bax? Should we leave?" Rena heard Julie call.

No reply.

"The main thing is to stay calm," George said.

Suddenly the lights blinked brightly, then stayed on.

Rena was the first to see it.

It was just a few feet away from her. Something large, something gray, swinging to and fro just off the floor.

She didn't scream. She was too horrified to scream when she realized it was Bax.

At first no one screamed. No one made a sound.

They saw the light cable, swung over a rafter. And they saw the large gray body, its neck bent at such an odd angle, attached to the cable.

No one believed it. No one could believe that Bax had done it, had hanged himself right in front of them.

13

"Is he dead?"

"Cut him down!"

"Oh, no! Oh, please—no!"

"Cut him down—somebody!"

"Get the nurse!"

"She's in town!"

"Put the chair under him!"

"Does he have a pulse?"

"Oh, no! *No* !"

"Look at his tongue!"

The horror of the sight in front of them divided into a dozen different horrors as each person in the theater tried to make sense of what he or she was seeing.

There was no way it could make sense.

There was no way that Bax really could be up there, hanging by the neck, his arms dangling at his sides, his tongue already purple and swollen, dark blood dripping down his chin.

"Cut him down! What are we waiting for?"

"Who has a knife?"

"You can't cut cable with a knife!"

"Is he dead? He isn't dead, is he?"

"Somebody call the police!"

"They won't get here for half an hour!"

"Cut him down!"

"Please—somebody—do something!"

Rena looked across the stage at George. He had dropped to his knees as if in prayer. She realized he was paralyzed there, paralyzed with revulsion and fear.

She stood up and walked quickly over to the hideous swaying figure in front of her. Someone reached out and handed her a pocket-knife. Would its blade be sharp enough? She had to try.

She reached up above Bax's tilted head, averting her eyes from the blood and the hideous swollen tongue, and began to slice the blade across the cable.

Harder. Faster. Faster still.

It seemed like an eternity. But it was only a few minutes later that the cable snapped and the heavy gray figure dropped facedown onto the floor. It seemed to bounce once, then lay unmoving, like one of those heavy scenery weight bags that always drop to the stage in bad movies.

"Is he dead?"

"Turn him over!"

"You turn him over!"

"Check to see if there's a pulse!"

"Give him mouth-to-mouth—quick!"

"Did anyone call the police?"

Rena was on her knees beside Bax's body now. And suddenly she was screaming. She didn't want to scream. She didn't remember starting to scream. She didn't even realize she was screaming.

It was too much. All too much.

Too much horror. Too much blood.

Too much blood in one lifetime. And too much death.

And so Rena screamed. And screamed. And screamed.

Bax sat up.

He pulled out the phony purple tongue.

He stared at Rena.

"That's the fear!" he proclaimed, grinning beneath his red-stained beard. "That's the fear! That's the feeling! You've got it now, Rena. You've got it."

Bax climbed to his feet. He seemed overjoyed. "Hold that feeling, everyone! Remember it!" he shouted happily, his voice echoing off the rafters.

14

The small theater reverberated with the sounds of the emotional reaction to Bax's ghastly performance. There were cries of disbelief, loud sighs, shouts of anger, sobbing, and wild, high-pitched laughter.

As the noise grew louder, Rena became silent.

She stopped screaming the moment Bax had decided to return to life. Now she was sitting on the hard stage floor, trembling all over, trembling with shock—and with rage.

She studied Bax's face, so pleased with himself, so overjoyed by the success of his performance, so completely self-obsessed.

Bax didn't care what he did to them, she realized.

More important, Bax would do *anything* to them. He would do anything to boost their performances.

Then Rena realized something more. Bax didn't do any of it for them. He did it all for himself. Boosting their performances, making them better actors, only reflected on him.

He didn't frighten them to improve them, Rena realized with sudden clarity, Bax frightened them because he enjoyed it.

He was cruel to them, he shocked them, he tortured them because he enjoyed it. He probably enjoyed it more than anything else he did, she realized, watching him, watching him beam with joy and satisfaction, almost ecstasy, as kids still cried and laughed and moaned, struggling to rid themselves of the hideous, terrifying scene he had just forced upon them.

He removed his handkerchief and wiped at the fake blood that had covered his chin and dripped down his beard. He didn't seem to realize that kids were truly upset, that some were sobbing, and some were in shock or sick.

None of that seemed to matter to him.

"Now you are all loose and relaxed!" he cried, stuffing the handkerchief back into his pants pocket. "Too bad that it took my suicide to get you that way!"

That was supposed to be a joke, but no one laughed.

Rena started to get up, but her legs were too trembly and weak. She sat back down on the stage.

Suddenly she felt an arm around her shoulders. Startled, she raised her head. It was Julie. She was wrapping a heavy cardigan around Rena's shoulders. "Are you okay? I heard you screaming."

"I—guess," Rena told her. If only she could stop trembling.

"You cut him down. You were so brave," Julie said.

"I was so stupid," Rena replied bitterly.

"You had no way of knowing," Julie assured her, talking softly, tying the sleeves of the cardigan across Rena's shoulders. "We were all paralyzed, but you acted. You should be proud of yourself."

"It was such a vicious thing for him to do," Rena said, feeling a little stronger, her anger making her strong. "So thoughtless, so selfish."

"Shhh. He'll hear you." Julie put her finger to her lips.

"I don't care. I really don't," Rena said, even louder.

"You'll be okay." Julie was trying hard to be sympathetic and reassuring. Somewhat to Rena's surprise, it seemed really genuine.

"There's enough real horror in this world," Rena said, not sure whether she was talking to Julie or herself. "There's enough real tragedy. Enough blood. Enough death."

"I think you now understand the feeling I want to achieve in *Curtains*," Bax was saying down in the auditorium. "Now we can begin."

Could Bax have killed the swan and put it in her bed? Rena asked herself. Yes, he could have.

Could Bax have slashed her clothes? Could Bax have switched the knives so that she stabbed Chip? Tapped on her window night after night so she got no sleep? Yes, he could have, she realized.

He was cruel enough.

He was uncaring enough.

He was obsessed with his play, with his work, with his success.

He could have, she realized. He could have.

But did he?

That was another question.

Did he?

Did he?

Why should she even have to ask that question?

What was she doing here?

"Rena," Bax repeated. Evidently he had been calling her for some time.

Rena stole a glance behind her. Julie was gone. She had returned to her seat without Rena realizing it.

"Rena," Bax said, a little more impatiently. "Are you ready to run through the scene the right way now? Are you ready to show me what you've learned tonight?"

"No," Rena said loudly. She climbed resolutely to her feet, tugging on the sleeves of the cardigan dangling in front of her.

"What?" Bax looked confused.

"I said no," Rena said. "No. No."

"Do you need a little time to compose your thoughts?" Bax asked, walking up to the stage, his hands on his hips. His beard was stained with narrow rivers of dried red stage blood.

"No," Rena repeated. "No, I don't."

"Well, what are you saying?" Bax asked, still bewildered.

"I'm saying that I'm not going to stay here and be a victim any longer!" Rena proclaimed.

A few kids gasped.

"Rena—" Bax started.

"It isn't worth it. None of it is worth it," Rena interrupted.

She had made her decision. She knew it was the right decision because she felt so much better, so much stronger the instant she made it.

"I'm quitting," she told Bax and everyone else. "I'm going home." She turned to the shocked kids watching her. "You're all crazy if you stay," she told them. "It isn't worth it. It just isn't worth it!"

"Stop, Rena! Stop right there!" Bax yelled.

She leapt off the stage and darted around him. Everyone was staring at her as she ran up the aisle.

Just don't trip, she told herself. Make this final exit a good one!

"Stop, Rena!" Bax was shouting. "Stop! My methods may be unorthodox. But I'm only trying to make a real actress of you! I'm only trying to get a good performance out of you!"

"Get it from Hedy!" Rena cried as she reached the door at the back of the theater. "I'm going home tomorrow!"

The cold night air felt so good. She felt so light, so free. She kept running, over the tall grass, up the hill, toward the dorm. She couldn't wait to pack up, to call her parents, to go home.

She had made a decision, a really tough decision. It was a decision never—never—to be a victim again. Now, for the first time in three years, she was beginning to feel strong again.

"Wait!" a voice called behind her.

Someone was running up the hill. "Wait! Rena, please wait!"

It was George. He caught up with her, breathing hard. "You can't leave," he said. It was more of a plea than a statement.

"Watch me," she replied.

"No. You can't. Rena, listen to me." He gently put a hand on her shoulder. "Please. Stay. I've—I really like you. I think we could be really good together. In the play—and in real life."

She hesitated for a moment, then stepped away. "That's the problem around here, George," she said. "No one seems to know the difference between the play and real life. No one seems to care about the difference between playacting and real life."

"But, Rena, we—"

"I can't deal with it, George. I have to know what's real and what isn't. It's very important to me. For reasons you can't understand."

"But I want to understand," George insisted.

"Goodbye," Rena said.

He looked positively heartbroken.

She ran past him, up the hill. She didn't turn back.

15

"Rena, I can't believe you're doing this," Julie said. They were walking back to the dorm after breakfast. The sun was pumpkin orange and still low in the morning sky. The tall grass was wet against their ankles.

Rena took a deep breath of fresh air. Everything seemed so fresh, so clear that morning. The whole world was brighter.

"I mean, I think I can understand it," Julie continued. "But I still don't believe you're leaving. You've got to change your mind."

Rena shook her head. Her hair was still wet from her shower. "Why do I have to change my mind?"

"Because you have to," Julie insisted.

"Well, I'm already packed, and I called my parents last night. They'll be here this morning. So I guess I couldn't change my mind even if I wanted to," Rena said all in one breath.

Julie pulled up a long strand of grass and began chewing on it as they walked. "But you can't let Hedy win," she said, waving to one of the boys from the set-design crew.

"This may be hard to understand," Rena said, "but I really don't see this as a defeat. I see it as a victory."

Julie pulled the blade of grass from between her teeth. "A victory?"

"That's right. I see it—"

"But, Rena, you're running away!"

"No. If I stayed here and went on as if nothing had happened, as if I still believed in the play, as if I still believed in Bax, in what I was doing here—then I'd be running away. I'd be running away from my true feelings, from what I really want. I'd be a victim, Julie. I'd be letting others control me. But I'm not doing that. I'm leaving because that's what I choose to do. And that's why I see it as a victory."

"Nice speech," Julie said sarcastically.

"What's your problem, Julie? Why are you giving me such a hard time this morning?"

Julie walked a few steps ahead. "I don't know. I guess I feel responsible. It was my idea to bring you here."

"But nothing that happened to me here was your fault," Rena said.

Or was it? she couldn't help thinking.

Was Julie making such a fuss about her leaving because she felt guilty for the things she had done to her?

No, Rena told herself. Stop thinking that way. She's just concerned about you. She just doesn't want you to make a wrong choice and be unhappy.

"Maybe I'll ask Bax if I can try out for the lead," Julie said, thinking out loud. "That might keep Hedy from getting it."

"I don't care about Hedy," Rena told her. "I really don't."

They went into their room. Julie opened the window to let some fresh air in. Rena packed a few final items into her trunk. The trunk was only half-filled, since most of her clothing had been slashed.

"Now what do we do? Sit around and stare at each other till your parents come?" Julie asked with an uncomfortable laugh.

"I think I want to take one last walk around," Rena said. "You know, just by myself. Maybe walk down by the water. It's so pretty here. I never really was in the mood to appreciate it."

She had to get out of that dorm room. Julie was getting on her nerves, and she didn't want anyone to spoil her good mood.

Julie acted a little hurt. But Rena figured she was probably relieved, too, that Rena was going out.

As she headed down the path toward the water, the sun was higher over the trees. It was going to be a hot day. She pulled off the light denim jacket she was wearing and tied it around her waist.

Except for a few kids hanging around the front of the theater, the camp seemed empty. Most kids were still eating breakfast in the mess hall. Some were sleeping late, since rehearsals didn't start until afternoon.

Rena was startled to see someone else heading down to the water. It was Hedy.

"Oh. You," Hedy said, rolling her eyes.

She was wearing a black bikini. Her hair was tucked into a white bathing cap.

Rena kept walking.

"I knew you couldn't stick it out," Hedy said, hurrying to keep up with her. "This isn't the place for you."

"No. It isn't," Rena agreed, walking even faster.

"I guess I'll have the role after all," Hedy said.

Rena turned suddenly to face her. Surprised, Hedy stumbled and almost fell over backward in the slippery grass. "How can you take any satisfaction in the role, knowing what you did to get it?" Rena cried.

"I don't know what you're talking about," Hedy said with exaggerated innocence.

"Yes, you do," Rena said, forcing herself to stay calm, forcing her voice to stay low and steady. "But you're too good an actress to let on."

"Thanks for the compliment," Hedy said sarcastically. "It means so much coming from you. And here's the nicest thing I'll ever say to you—goodbye!" She turned and, evidently forgetting about her swim, stomped back up the hill.

"Break a leg!" Rena called after her. She was pleased to get the last word in, but it wasn't much of a victory.

She hates me, Rena thought, continuing down the path. Someone I hardly know really hates me. And all because of a silly part in a silly summer-camp play.

She could see the boathouse now at the end of the small, rickety dock. And she could hear the waves of the sound splashing and churning onto the sandy shore. The tide was coming in.

I should have put on a bathing suit, she thought. I could have taken one last swim.

She made her way more carefully as the hill grew steeper and sandier. Two gulls floated lazily in the clear sky above. It's so beautiful here, she told herself. What a shame I never noticed till now.

The splash of the waves grew louder. Suddenly she heard a sound behind her. A cracking twig. Running footsteps.

Someone was coming after her.

16

"George! What are you doing down here?" she cried.

It took him a while to catch his breath. He was wearing blue sweatpants and a gray sleeveless T-shirt. The front of the T-shirt was stained with sweat.

"I've been running," he said finally, brushing back his wet black hair with his hand. "I run every morning. I was near the path. I heard your conversation with Hedy."

"I guess you could call it a conversation," Rena said bitterly.

"She had no right to talk to you that way," George said heatedly.

"Go tell her." Rena turned away from him and headed for the dock.

Why did he haunt her? she asked herself. Why couldn't he leave her alone? She had hoped to get away from the camp without having to see him again, without having to say goodbye. But there he was, loping along beside her, his dark eyes looking for something in hers, something they weren't about to find.

"I—I just wanted to walk. You know. Be by myself," she said, not wanting to hurt his feelings, but hoping he'd take the hint just the same.

"Come with me," he said softly. He took her hand. His hand was hot and wet. "I want to show you something beautiful. In the boathouse. It might cheer you up."

She pulled back. "I don't really need to be cheered up."

He tightened his grip. "Come on anyway," he said, laughing. "You'll like this."

"Bax said not to go into the boathouse," she said warily.

"We'll only stay a minute." He pulled her onto the dock, and she relented.

The boards of the dock creaked beneath their feet as they walked. The boathouse swayed and bobbed up and down as the waves grew higher. It smelled of fish and mildew and decaying wood.

George struggled to pull open the thick door, which was heavy and warped so that it slid only with great effort, and they stepped inside. He was still holding her hand.

Rotting, broken canoes bobbed up and down inside, banging noisily together as the water swirled in, then out. The far end, usually open to the bay, had been boarded up to keep any new boats from getting in. Light streamed in from an enormous jagged hole in the arched roof. Wooden stairs, most of them broken or missing, led to a storage area above their heads. The smell of rotting fish and mildew grew stronger.

"Let's get out of here. This place is creepy," Rena whispered. "What do you want to show me?"

"Over here," he whispered back, pulling her across the warped wooden floorboards. He pulled her to the edge, where the floor ended and the water began. "Look. Here." He pointed down.

There, tucked in the back of a bobbing canoe, was a perfectly round nest of twigs and tree bark, filled with baby robins. They had their heads up and their mouths open, squeaking and squealing for their mother, who was probably out finding food for them.

"How sweet," Rena said. "You're right. This did cheer me up. They're so adorable."

George grinned and squeezed her hand.

He isn't such a bad guy, Rena thought. I've really been unfair to him.

"Sit down for just a minute," George said, dropping down to the floor, letting his feet dangle over the side.

The water was inching higher. It was nearly up to George's running shoes.

"We really shouldn't stay," Rena said uneasily. But she sat down beside him anyway. "It was nice of you to show me the baby robins."

"I wanted to show you a lot of things," he said wistfully, staring down into the water.

"I-I'm sorry things didn't work out," Rena said.

"Things usually don't work out for me," he said with unusual bitterness. "It seems to be the story of my life."

Rena realized she didn't know anything about his life. That night they had sneaked out, he said he was poor. That was about all she knew about him.

"I haven't had a happy life," he continued as if reading her thoughts. "In fact, a lot of bad things have happened to me. Someone I really loved was killed. It changed me. For good. Nothing has been the same since."

"I'm sorry," she said. She felt foolish. It was such an inadequate reply. But what was she supposed to say?

Why was he telling her this?

In a few hours she'd be gone, away from camp, away from him. She'd probably never see him again.

He pulled his feet up and scooted back. The water had risen almost up to floor level. "The tide's coming in fast," he said, watching the bobbing canoes. "It's kind of exciting, don't you think? You really feel like you're in a different world. You feel far from everyone, from everything."

"George, let's go," she pleaded.

He looked hurt. "Please, Rena. I know you're going home today. Won't you stay with me just a little longer? Look."

He pointed to the canoe with the nest. The mother bird had returned carrying a long, squirming earthworm. The baby robins squealed even louder, grabbing at the worm with their tiny pointed beaks.

"I really want to get out of here," Rena said, climbing to her feet. "Come on. The water's getting higher."

She saw a large black rat hop from canoe to canoe. The canoes bobbed more violently, banging together as the water rose. The rat made its way excitedly from boat to boat. Rena saw another rat, even larger, hopping after it.

"I just want to get out of here!" she cried.

"Okay, okay," George said, unable to hide his unhappiness. "I just thought we'd talk for a little while. That's all. You're nervous a lot of the time, aren't you?"

She didn't reply. How was she supposed to answer a question like that? He didn't really want an answer. He was just being unpleasant.

Glancing back at the two scampering rats, she followed close behind George as they made their way to the boathouse door. He turned the metal knob and pushed.

Then he pushed again, a little harder.

He tried once again, turning the knob as far as it would move and leaning into the thick wooden door with his shoulder.

Then he tried turning the knob in the other direction.

Then he tried pulling on the door instead of pushing it.

When he turned back to Rena, he had a very worried expression on his face. "The door's locked," he said. "Someone has locked us in!"

17

"George, that's not funny!" Rena cried.

The water lapped at her sneakers. The tide was coming in faster. The entire boathouse rocked and swayed against the dock as the murky brown waters rose.

The expression on George's face told Rena he wasn't joking. His eyes were wild with fright, and his mouth was set in a determined line.

He jiggled the doorknob frantically, trying it in one direction, then the other. He lowered his shoulder and shoved against the door with all his might.

"No!" he cried out as his feet slipped out from under him and he fell on the wet floorboards. "Getting slippery," he said, climbing back up and resuming his efforts.

"The water's up to my ankles," Rena cried. "We've got to get out of here fast. Can't you break the door down?"

"No. The wood is too thick," he said. "Maybe I can

find a weak spot in the wall. But it's hard to get a grip."

The cold water crept up past Rena's ankles. She looked for a higher place to stand, but there was none.

"What's that clicking sound?" she asked, trying not to sound as frightened as she felt.

She turned around and saw the answer to her own question. The clicking was the sound of rats' feet. At least a dozen large black rats were scampering excitedly from one rotting canoe to another as the waters rose.

"George—the rats—"

"Just ignore them. Maybe they'll ignore us. The tide sure comes in fast. I—"

He didn't finish what he was saying because the entire boathouse suddenly lurched to the right, throwing them both to the floor.

The rats began to squeal and hop faster from boat to boat. Rena jumped up quickly. The brown water was up to her knees.

She ran over to George and grabbed his shoulder. "George, if we don't get out, we're going to drown!"

"Don't worry. We'll get out." His words sounded brave, but his frightened face told a different story.

"Hedy!" Rena shouted suddenly. "Hedy! Let us out!"

There was no reply.

"You think Hedy locked us in?" George asked, surprised.

The water was above their knees.

Rena realized she'd have to scream louder to be heard over the screeching of the rats and the roar of the swirling water.

"Hedy!" she shouted, cupping her hands over her

mouth. "Let us out! You've got the part! I'm going home! What more do you want?"

They listened for a reply, for a sound, for any sign that another human was nearby.

Silence.

"Is anybody out there?" George called, his voice cracking. "Can anybody hear us?"

Silence.

"Hedy, let us out!" Rena cried. "Hedy, we're going to drown in here!"

The commotion excited the rats. The high-pitched squeals became higher-pitched. As the canoes bobbed more violently in the churning water, the rats became more daring, leaping higher, scampering across a boat quickly, then plunging over the side, up into the air, onto the next boat.

"Hedy, please!" Rena was begging now. The water was nearly up to her waist.

The rotting rafters above them creaked and groaned. The boathouse shifted to the left, then swayed to the right again.

"Hedy, I'm in here too!" George shouted. "It's me! George! Hedy, let us out! Let us *out!*"

Again, the only reply was the shrill squeals of the scampering rats.

"Why is she doing this?" Rena cried, no longer able to keep the fear out of her voice. "Does she really want to kill us both?"

George shrugged. "You tell me." He sounded more angry than frightened.

"Try again. The door. Try to push it." Rena's mind was swirling like the water, and her panic was rising just as rapidly.

"The water's too high. It's hard to get any balance." George put his shoulder to the door, but his feet went out from under him. He splashed back up.

"Hedy! Hedy! Let us out!" Rena screamed.

George tried pushing again, then slipped again.

A rat hopped onto his shoulder. It stood there, balanced on its two hind legs.

"No! Get off! Get off!" Rena shrieked.

The rat squealed in George's ear, then dived off into a canoe. George shuddered, slipped again, tried to regain his footing, but fell face-forward into the water.

The water crept up above Rena's waist. It felt ice-cold. The thick mud it carried clung to her legs and her shorts.

She bumped up against the door—

And to her surprise, the door moved.

The door was open.

The door wasn't locked.

George was still splashing in the water, trying to regain his feet.

Rena's heart pounded with happiness, with relief. For a moment she was too stunned to speak.

"George—" she said finally. She wanted to tell him the good news.

But then something made her stop.

A frightening thought made her stop.

"George," she called, putting the fear back in her voice. He regained his feet and, wet and mud-soaked, pulled himself forward to rejoin her. "George, try the door again. Please!"

"Okay. Maybe this time," he said, shaking water from his hair, then wiping his eyes with his hands. "Maybe she'll open this time."

He tried the doorknob again, first slowly, then with angry desperation. He put his shoulder against the door and pushed once again. The door didn't budge.

He turned to her, his face revealing total panic, total resignation. "It's still locked, Rena. What are we going to do?"

Now she knew.

She knew that he was lying.

The door wasn't locked. The door was open.

They could step out the door, step out of the boathouse, step out of this terrifying nightmare.

George was acting. It was all a performance.

But why?

Was he really trying to kill them both?

Or just her?

18

"What are we going to do?" George cried, his eyes darting crazily back and forth, the water creeping halfway up his chest.

"You shouldn't go over the top with your eyes like that," Rena told him, moving purposefully to the door.

"What? What do you mean?" He looked confused.

"You should be able to convey fear with your body. You shouldn't rely on exaggerated eye movements. At least that's what Bax would say."

"Rena, are you okay? You're not making any sense." He was staring into her eyes now, trying to figure out why she had changed, why she no longer looked frightened, why she suddenly seemed so in control.

"Just keep calm," he said, resuming his performance. "We'll find a way out. There's got to be a way out."

The boathouse shifted again. The rafters above

them cracked as they swayed. The rats continued their frenzied hopping.

"I know the way out, George," Rena said, staring back into his eyes for the first time. "I know the way out, and I'm gone!"

She reached for the doorknob and pushed the door open a bit.

He grabbed her arm.

"Let go, George. I'm going out that door."

He squeezed her wrist tighter and jerked her back. "You're not leaving, Rena. You're never leaving." His face went blank. His eyes narrowed in hatred.

She struggled to free herself. "What's the matter with you?"

"We're going to die here. Both of us."

A rat hopped onto George's shoulder, then leapt for a canoe hung over their heads. The rat missed the canoe, hit the water with a splash, and disappeared beneath the murky surface.

"George, don't be crazy—"

He pulled her arm violently. She lurched backward and lost her footing. She struggled back to her feet, choking on the filthy water.

"I'm not crazy," he said, staring into her eyes with a cold fury she'd never seen before. "I know what I'm doing. I've known since the beginning."

"The beginning? What are you talking about?"

"Since camp started. I've known. I've known what I had to do, Rena."

"But you—we—"

"I've known what to do, and I've done it. I'm the one, Rena. I'm the one who killed the swan. I'm the one who tapped on your window. I'm the one who switched the knives. It was so easy. I was prop master, remember? I'm the one, Rena. The one who's been doing all those terrible things to you."

Rena turned her head as the drowned rat floated past them.

When she turned back, George was still staring at her, unblinking, his face twisted in anger.

"But why, George? Why did you do those things to me?" She tried to pull away, but his grip was too tight.

The boathouse swayed. The rafters creaked and shifted.

"Because I'm not George," he said.

With his free hand he pulled the jacket off his waist. He held it up so she could see the initials once again. A.M.

"A.M., Rena. A.M.," he repeated. "I'm not George. I'm Andy. Andy Malone."

"Malone?"

The name sent a shiver to her heart.

"That's right," he said, his face twitching. "That's right. Didn't you guess? Couldn't you see?"

"You're—"

"I'm Kenny's brother. Kenny's brother from California."

Rena stared at him as if seeing him for the first time. Yes. He did look like Kenny. Like a darker version of Kenny.

"You killed Kenny, Rena. And I came all the way here to kill you." His voice cracked. His face twitched. Rena could see that he was completely out of control now.

"George—Andy—let go. My wrist. You're hurting me."

He didn't respond to her plea. He stared at her, breathing heavily.

"Andy, how did you know I'd be here at this camp?" she asked, trying to keep him talking. If she could keep him talking, maybe he'd loosen his grip and she could escape.

"Friends of Kenny told me where you were," he said. "Kenny had friends, you know. He had friends. And he had a brother who loved him. Even though I lived three thousand miles away. I miss him, Rena. I miss him so much!"

"I miss him too!" Rena screamed.

The boathouse rocked low to the right. Some boards plummeted down from the rafters, smashing into the canoes below.

"Andy, we've got to get out of here. It's collapsing!"

He jerked her forward, tightening his grip on her arm. "Goodbye, Rena," he said, a smile spreading across his face, a triumphant smile, a satisfied smile. "Goodbye."

He grabbed her head with both hands and pulled it under the water.

She tried to free herself by flailing out with her arms. But he held on, pushing her head down, keeping her underwater.

She stopped resisting and dived deeper instead, grabbing his legs with both hands, pulling him off-balance, pulling him underwater too.

Trying to save himself, trying to get back up to the surface, he let go of her. It was the result she had hoped for. She darted away from him, swimming quickly in the thick, churning water.

He dived after her. He grabbed her arm, but she slipped away.

She heard a cracking sound, followed by a low rumble.

The boathouse was collapsing on top of them.

Sputtering and choking, unable to see clearly because of the filthy water, Rena swam toward the doorway.

She turned as she reached the door. Andy was close behind, swimming fast, closing the gap between them.

"Oh, no!"

She screamed as a rafter dropped. It hit Andy on the head, then ricocheted into the water.

She saw his eyes go wide, his mouth drop open.

Then she saw his eyes roll back in his head.

He slumped forward, facedown in the water. His arms floated up to the surface. His body bobbed with the waves.

With a loud crack, the rest of the boathouse collapsed and fell away from the dock.

Rena dived down into the water as the boathouse hit the surface. Then, swimming hard, she plunged free of the tangle of boards and rotting canoes. She swam to the shore and with a grateful, relieved sigh pulled herself onto the beach.

"Andy, where are you? Andy!"

She saw his body less than twenty yards from shore, bobbing facedown in the waves.

19

She was back in Kenny's basement.

The rec room was brighter than she remembered it. Brighter and clearer. She could see everything now.

The shock of seeing Kenny's brother bobbing so lifelessly in the water brought it back, a flash of memory, so brief yet so perfectly clear.

"Take the gun," Kenny told her. "Spin the cylinder." He shoved the revolver at her.

"No." She refused. "No, put it away."

He shoved the gun at her again. "Take it. Take it."

"No." She refused again.

She turned away from Kenny. She ran. She ran from the room. She knew she had to get help.

Then she heard the gunshot.

It was all so clear now.

Three years later, it was so clear.

She heard the gunshot. She was on the stairs, running for help.

She wasn't in the room.

134

She had never even touched the gun.

Kenny did it all.

So clear now.

Kenny did it. Kenny killed himself. And the horror of the moment had clouded her memory for three years.

Now Kenny's brother, Andy, floated facedown in the water, bobbing with the current like a piece of driftwood, his arms floating lifelessly on top of the waves.

She had to save him. At least she had to try.

She pulled off her wet sneakers. They seemed to weigh a hundred pounds each. Taking a deep breath, she ran into the onrushing waves. The current was stronger than she thought. Even though the tide was coming in, she could feel a powerful undertow, pulling her first to the left, then out from the shore.

When the choppy brown water was up over her knees, she plunged in and began to swim. Where was Andy? She raised her head to look for him and was startled by a huge wave that crashed over her head, tossing her back, invading her nose and mouth. She choked, struggled to see, dived beneath another wave, then surfaced, still choking, her nose and eyes burning.

She could see him now, floating on top of the water. The current was carrying him away from her. He was farther away than before.

I've got to get there. I've got to get there. The words repeated in her mind as she pulled herself over the water, her heart pounding, her muscles beginning to ache with each stroke.

I've got to get there, got to get there.

But what if he was already dead?

No. He couldn't be. He couldn't.

Stay alive, Andy. Stay alive. I'm coming for you.

No more death. I've had enough death already. We've had enough death already.

Please, please stay alive.

She saw his body sink below the water. His head dropped. His arms slowly followed him down.

"No!" she cried aloud, and began to swim faster, her arms splashing frantically, her feet kicking hard, harder, propelling her forward.

The ache in her side grew to a throbbing pain.

She ignored it, plunging forward, her strokes as frenzied as her thoughts.

Please don't die. Please.

As if her words had summoned him back, he floated up to the surface. She was closer, closer. The pain wouldn't quit. The pain was slowing her, stopping her. The pain was taking over now. . . .

But she was there.

And she grabbed him.

She grabbed his head and pulled it out of the water, turned, breathing hard, breathing happily, the pain subsiding as she faced the shore and started to swim back, her cargo in tow.

Was he alive?

She couldn't tell.

A few minutes later she dragged him onto the wet sand. She spread him out on his back. His body offered no resistance. His eyes were closed. His mouth hung open. Bending over him, she pumped his chest. Water sprayed from his mouth.

Was he alive?

Was he alive?

Could she make him alive?

She kept pushing on his chest, pumping rhythmically, trying to remember how it was done in lifesaving class. Then she pried open his mouth and started to give him mouth-to-mouth.

An eternity later, he moved.

His arms flew up. He tried to push her away.

"Don't make me live!" he cried. "I just want to die!"

"Andy, you're going to be okay! You're going to be okay!"

His arms fell back to the sand. He was breathing steadily now.

Rena turned around to see Julie and Marcie running down the hill toward her. She leapt to her feet and waved her arms.

"Here you are!" Julie cried. "What happened to you? I was so worried. You didn't come back from your walk."

"We looked everywhere," Marcie cried.

"Your parents are here," Julie said. Then she saw the figure lying on the beach. "Oh, my Lord! George! Is he—is he—"

"He's going to be okay, I think," Rena told her. She slumped to her knees, her weariness catching up with her. The fear, the overwhelming fear, was upon her at once. She shook it away. She had saved Andy, and she was alive. She wasn't going to give in now.

"He isn't George," she told them. "He just made up the name George."

"Rena, what do you mean?" Julie was totally confused.

"He's Andy. Kenny's brother."

"You mean—"

Rena nodded.

Julie threw her arms around Rena and hugged her.

"He tried to kill me," Rena told her. "He's the one who's been torturing me all this time."

"Go get Bax," Julie told Marcie. "Call the police. Get someone down here."

Marcie turned and ran up the hill.

"Are you okay?" Julie asked, wiping mud off Rena's cheek.

Rena smiled. She took a deep breath. "Yes," she said. "Yes. I think I'm going to be fine!"

"I don't believe a thing that's happened here," Rena's father said, struggling to drag her trunk to the door of the dorm room.

"Give her a break," Rena's mother chided him. She gave Rena an indulgent smile. "She'll explain it all again when she's ready."

"But I just don't believe it," her father repeated.

"It's a weird story, all right," Rena said, squeezing past her mother to make sure she hadn't forgotten anything in the closet.

"I never thought this theater camp was for her in the first place," her father said, groaning from the weight of the trunk.

All in all, Rena told herself, her parents had been very understanding. After all, they had driven all the way to the camp on a day's notice, only to find her drenched and bedraggled, exhausted, half-drowned, and covered in mud.

Her mother had been horrified. Her father had just frowned and shaken his head. "Looks like the outdoor life doesn't agree with you," he had cracked.

Rena couldn't believe how happy she was to see them both. She couldn't believe how good she felt about everything. Her memory was clear. The sadness remained. But the guilt had been washed away forever. Three years of horror were now over for her, she realized, and Andy would soon get the help he needed.

As they walked to the car, her mother put her arm around Rena's shoulder. "Rena, why are you leaving camp early?" she asked, whispering the question in Rena's ear.

"I don't belong in the theater," Rena replied, smiling and putting her arm around her mother's waist. "I like the real world better."

Her mother studied her, surprised.

"I think I'm going to like the real world from now on," Rena said brightly.

She slipped away from her mother and climbed quickly into the backseat of the car. She couldn't believe how much she was looking forward to the long ride home.

About the Author

"Where do you get your ideas?"

That's the question that R. L. Stine is asked most often. "I don't know where my ideas come from," he says. "But I do know that I have a lot more scary stories in my mind that I can't wait to write."

So far, he has written nearly three dozen mysteries and thrillers for young people, all of them bestsellers.

Bob grew up in Columbus, Ohio. Today he lives in an apartment near Central Park in New York City with his wife, Jane, and fourteen-year-old son, Matt.